# Deadline

Thomas Erwin and T.M.Erwin

Published by T.M.Erwin, 2024.

This is a work of fiction. Similarities to real people, places, or events are entirely coincidental.

DEADLINE

**First edition. June 13, 2024.**

Copyright © 2024 Thomas Erwin and T.M.Erwin.

ISBN: 979-8227816535

Written by Thomas Erwin and T.M.Erwin.

# Deadline

# Prologue

It was Mary Lewis' birthday, and she was very happy. She had just finished shopping for new clothes on Rodeo Drive and was having lunch and drinks with her two best friends at Del Marco's, one of the nicer restaurants in Los Angeles. Happy and content, she said goodbye to her friends at the restaurant before heading to the parking ramp where she had earlier parked her new baby blue Corvette, a birthday gift from her husband. Leaving the parking ramp, she enjoyed the drive home with the convertible top down, soaking up the dry air under the warm California sun.

Arriving at her home in Beverly Hills, she pulled into the large circular driveway of the mansion where she noticed that the combination marble Roman water fountain and koi fish pond in the middle of the driveway was hardly showing any water volume through the fountain's orifices.

*The damn water intake must be plugged up again. I guess I'll have to tell Hector clean it out again. This was the third time it had happened this month,* she thought to herself.

She parked her car in the driveway next to the four-car garage and exited the vehicle. Then taking one long last look at her new Corvette, headed into the house. Entering the front foyer through a set of heavily carved oak doors, she placed her car keys into the silver tray resting on the Italian marble top credenza located on the side of the foyer. She then placed her packages containing her purchases on the floor.

"Maria, I'm home. Will you come and get my bags and put them in my bedroom?" she called out, her voice echoing back at her from the tall foyer ceiling. No one replied, and no one came to assist her.

*That's strange. I wonder where everybody is?* she thought to herself, slightly irritated but determined to not let anything like a missing servant ruin her special day.

Walking past the foyer and into the mansion's great room, she noticed the sliding glass doors that led outside to the Olympic size swimming pool were wide open. Looking around and seeing no one, she walked across the great room to the other side, to check and see if her husband was outside by the pool, her high heels making a staccato rhythm on the marble floor as she walked to the pool area.

Walking through the open sliding doors, she passed by the marble Roman columns and statuary toward the swimming pool. Initially not seeing anyone, she called out. "Honey, I'm home. Can I give you a fashion show of the new wardrobe I bought today?" No reply. "Hank. Are you out here?" she questioned, walking closer to the pool. Then she stopped dead in her tracks. Through horrified eyes, she saw the bodies of her husband wearing a swimming suit and the maid, Maria, fully dressed, both floating face down in the swimming pool, their blood slowly mingling together, staining the crystal-clear pool water.

Horrified, she screamed and started to run to her husband, praying that she wasn't too late to save him, when someone from behind her delivered a staggering blow to the side of her head. Semi-conscious, she fell onto her knees and tried to support herself. Then a loud boom echoed in her ears as a sharp searing pain entered her back as the whole world around her turned into darkness.

# Chapter 1

Maxine Somers lay in her bed, listening to the sound of a fire truck's siren as it raced past her apartment building. It had been a short night as she had worked a double shift at the 37th Precinct station house in downtown Los Angeles, and it had been a very busy night.

She looked across the double bed at the empty spot next to her. She still was not entirely used to sleeping alone. The divorce from her second husband had been finalized only ten days ago, and even though he had been kicked out of her apartment over half a year ago, she was still having a hard time adjusting to being single again.

Alexandria, her daughter by her first husband, was studying at Berkeley on a full scholarship and living on campus. Fortunately for Maxine, her daughter inherited looks from her mother and her brains from her first husband, and most fortunately, not from the cretin whom she had recently divorced. Her daughter had warned her repeatedly that her second husband was no good, but Max, in her stubbornness, had refused to see it.

She felt relief that the part of her life with her second husband was over. She knew she should never have taken up with him, but he caught and took advantage of her at a very vulnerable time in her life. Her first husband, who was in the military, had passed away after being seriously wounded in

Afghanistan. She also began drinking heavily to dull the pain of her loss.

Her second husband was a user and abuser. He couldn't hold down a steady job but found a steady cash flow and drinking partner in Maxine. When drunk, he would take out his frustrations with his fists, usually in a bar fight and sometimes on Maxine. Of course, he was always sorry after sobering up, relying on her to get him out of jail after the bar fights and begging her to take him back when he used her as his punching bag. It wasn't until she couldn't hide the bruises anymore that she had to tell her precinct captain what was happening to her at home.

Captain McDaniel took her under his wing by helping her to get into counseling. He acted as her sponsor at the Alcoholics Anonymous program and even found her a good divorce attorney.

Max appreciated McDaniel's help and tried her best to live up to his expectations, but she fell off the wagon several times before she was emotionally stable enough to make the program work. She hadn't had a drink for over six months and was feeling stronger every day. Now she was finally sober and single.

The night before, Captain McDaniel had asked her to check in with him when she came into work at the start of her next shift. Max got out of bed, slid the sheet and coverlet up to the head board and threw the pillow over them. She walked into the apartment's kitchenette and made herself a pot of coffee and some toast for her breakfast, enjoying her quiet time while it lasted. Looking around her apartment, she realized how drab and dingy it looked. She realized that it had needed a new coat of paint for several years, but she was enough of a realist to know the company that owned the apartment building wouldn't put in any money into improving or upgrading the property. She didn't want to put any of her funds into it, but the rent was right.

After finishing her breakfast, she took a quick shower, dressed into her police uniform and headed down from her apartment building in the elevator. Hitting the street, she walked down the block until she reached the lot where her car was parked. Pulling out of the parking lot, she headed down the street to her precinct building,

Traffic was light on the street leading to her work but as she drove over the Golden State Freeway overpass, she observed the traffic below was fully stopped and was completely backed up for as far as she could see. She knew that this was a normal traffic day for a typical Los Angeles work- day morning and silently complained about all of the population in the city.

Arriving at the precinct building, she parked her car in the employee parking garage and walked into the offices of the 37th Precinct Police Department where she had worked for the last seven years. After getting out of the Army, she signed up for the Police Academy and although almost twenty women started the course, she was one of only three women in her graduating class.

Entering the break room she saw her patrol partner, Jerry Sanders, standing with several other officers by the coffee pot. She acknowledged him with a nod of her head, and he reciprocated back.

"Hey partner, need some drain cleaner to start the day?" he asked, pointing at the pot of coffee on top of the countertop.

Max shook her head and said, "Boss wants to see me first thing this morning, but please save me a donut, will you?"

"You in trouble again?" Sanders jokingly kidded her.

"Yeah, you know me. The big troublemaker." She countered as she headed towards her captain's office. As she approached his glassed-in office, she observed another man in the office having a conversation with her captain. The unknown man was wearing a suit and tie as opposed to the captain's uniform worn by McDaniel's.

Knocking on the door, both men turned. Captain McDaniel signaled her to enter. Entering the office, she noticed that both men had scowls on their faces.

*Oh no! Maybe I am in trouble.* She thought, quickly going through her mind as to what she might have done wrong,

"Officer Somers, I don't know if you've met Deputy Chief Johnson from Central. He's here because of a complaint against you." Captain McDaniel explained, looking sternly at her.

Max felt the bottom of her stomach drop as she raced through her mind, trying to recall what she might have done to draw a complaint. "A complaint against me, Sir?" She squeaked out to Chief Johnson.

"Yes Officer Somers, and it is a very serious matter. The complaint concerns you and the Police Department dress code policy. Even now, I see you're out of compliance." Chief Johnson sternly stated.

Max quickly looked over her uniform to see what was out of compliance. Not seeing anything that warranted a complaint, she asked, "I'm sorry, Sir, but I don' see what is out of compliance."

"I'm not going to explain why you're not in dress code. You should know the regulations by now, so I am going to have to ask for your shield, Officer Somers.

Now pure panic and confusion rocked Max to her very core. Confused and embarrassed, she slowly removed the silver badge from her uniform and respectfully placed it on the desk in front of her. She felt tears started to well up in her eyes as she anticipated what she felt was the inevitable outcome. Captain McDaniel picked up the badge and threw it disdainfully into his desk drawer and slammed it shut. The loud sound of the drawer slamming shut snapped Max's mind back to her reality. She quickly dried her eyes with her sleeve, not wanting to give them the satisfaction of seeing her cry.

"How do you want to handle this Chief Johnson?" McDaniel's asked.

"I don't know," he replied, "Maybe I can have her put this on." Chief Johnson replied. With that statement, he took a small box out of his suit pocket. Opening it up, he took out a gold badge and pinned it onto Max's uniform, in the spot where her silver one had just been removed.

Max needed a moment to mentally process what had just happened. Finally cognizant of what was happening and realizing that she wasn't being fired, a slow smile slowly slid across her face. "I must passed the detective exam, didn't I?" she exclaimed excitedly.

Chief Johnson was the first to respond. "Yes, you did, and you had one of the higher scores in this years testing group." He told her as he eagerly took her hand and shook it.

"Sorry about the hazing, Detective Somers, but it's kind of a ritual in command when we promote someone from patrol to detective. I hope you'll forgive us." Captain McDaniel asked of her.

"No problem, Captain. I'll try and make you proud." Max told him.

"You already have," McDaniel replied, "You held up to the hazing well. Some of the men blubber like babies when we pull this stunt on them. However, I must insist that this ritual stays a secret between just us. If you blab this to the other officers, we might have to pull your shield for real," he told her with a sly smile.

"No problem, Captain. You secret is good with me." Max reassured him.

"Good. Now get out of here. Go show your new shield to your buddies out there. we'll do the photos later," he told her, pointing out at the squad room.

"Thank you, Captain and thank you, Chief Johnson." Max gushed as she shook both of their hands, then headed for the door.

"Don't forget to wear street clothes tomorrow and see me first thing in the morning and we'll talk about your re-assignment," McDaniel told her.

"Will do, Captain." Max responded as she eagerly headed out of the office, looking for Jerry Sanders and her other friends.

# Chapter 2

Max awoke to the sounds of the next-door neighbors fighting, again. The thin apartment walls didn't do much to mute the sounds of their shouting and the loud television. As she laid in her bed, she heard the man screaming and then the front door of the next door apartment slamming. Silence followed for a few moments until she could hear the woman begin sobbing on the other side of her bedroom wall.

Max had been living in her apartment almost four years, but her neighbor had only been there for about six months. The woman had moved in first, then the man had arrived about two months later. Max felt sorry for the woman since she had been in her situation too, but from past occurrences when she tried to mediate between them, she was met with insults and anger by both the man and the woman.

After the second time she tried to intervene, she realized it would only be a manner of time before someone would be seriously injured or worse. She could only wait for that day to occur, and prayed that the consequences wouldn't be fatal.

Dressing for work, it felt strange to her not putting on her uniform. After dressing in a pair of black dress slacks and a dress shirt, she clipped her new gold shield onto her belt. Looking at herself in the mirror, she realized that she could get used to not wearing her uniform to work.

Arriving at the 37th Precinct building, she headed immediately toward McDaniel's office. Reaching the office door, McDaniel saw her through the glass partition and signaled immediately for her to enter. Walking in, he motioned to her to take a seat, Max saw a leather couch up against a wall and a wooden chair in front of his desk. She chose the chair. After she was seated, McDaniel leaned back in his swivel chair, put his hands behind his head, smiled and asked her. "How do you feel about Beverly Hills?"

"Nice place to visit but I can't afford to live there." Max shot back with a grin on her face.

"Understood, neither can I but I'd like try it someday." McDaniel told her. Max nodded her head in agreement, wondering where the conversation was heading.

McDaniel sat forward in his chair and picked up a manila folder from his desk. "I got what you might call a request from Central. They need a detective replacement at the Beverly Hills station. They're down one due to reassignment. Are you interested?" McDaniel asked.

Max didn't even have to think about it. "I'll take it," she responded immediately.

"Are you sure you don't want to think about it overnight?" He questioned pensively.

"No, I don't have to think about it at all. Can I start today?" Max quickly asked.

"A real eager beaver, aren't you. They're really going to love you in Beverly Hills. Okay, I'll notify your new captain that you'll be coming over. Your new boss is John O'Brien. You will however, need to go over to Central and fill out your new transfer paperwork with Human Resources," he explained to her.

"Sure thing. Could you tell Captain O'Brien that I'll be able to report to him around noon?" Max requested.

"I'll call him before you leave the building, but before you leave, I just want to warn you about something. The 48$^{th}$ in Beverly Hills is a little, how should I say this, it's kind of eccentric. I think it's what I would call a different mind set and clientele. Are you sure you still want to go there?" He asked her.

"I don't care if they have space aliens as clientele." Max jokingly replied.

Captain McDaniel laughed out loud and told her, "Okay, head on out to Central and do your paperwork, and good luck. Go make me proud."

"Thank you, Sir." Max responded, as she headed out the door. "I will."

It took her the better part of two hours, between waiting and filling out the transfer paperwork, and an interview with a HR person, before she was done at Central.

It took her almost forty minutes of driving around downtown Beverley Hills, for her to find the 48$^{th}$ precinct. Not because she got lost but because she drove past it several times before she realized that it was in a modern five-story office building with no signage on the exterior designating it as a police station.

Parking her car at an available parking spot in front of the building, she fed the parking meter with enough coins to give her the maximum two-hour limit and proceeded into the building. Walking into the mezzanine and past a receptionist, she proceeded to the elevator and read the directory on the wall next to the elevator door. The sign read –

Parking-basement, Lobby-first floor, Evidence, Forensic and Morgue-second floor, Beverly Hills Police Department-third floor, Booking and Jail- fourth floor, Administrative-fifth floor. Entering the elevator, Max pushed the fifth-floor button.

The elevator took a half a minute to get her to the top floor. Stepping out onto the fifth floor, she was impressed with the overall appearance of efficiency and proficiency. The room was divided up into a multitude of cubicles with people coming and going, back and forth, each person carrying out whatever task they were working on.

Looking around, trying to figure out where to report in, she was approached by an older, unshaven man wearing jeans and a Grateful Dead tee shirt with a gold shield clipped on his belt.

"You lost, Missy?" He asked gruffly.

"Looking for Captain O'Brien. I was just transferred in this precinct from the 37$^{th}$," she explained to him.

He gave her a once overlook from her head to her toes. She had on a black pair of slacks and a white button-up blouse, buttoned all the way up to the neck. "O'Brien's office is all the way to your left. You'll see the sign on his door when you get closer. Can I give you a little head up, though?" He asked her.

"Sure," Max replied sheepishly.

"Loosen up those top two or three buttons on your blouse, and you and O'Brien will get along just fine," he told her with a subtle smile.

Max was somewhat shocked at his advice. Slightly blushing, she immediately moved her hand to her neck, feeling her buttons. "Thanks," she replied, then added. "I guess I can use all the help I can get. By the way, I'm Detective Maxine

Somers," she told him, extending her hand to him. He looked at her extended hand and then shook it once. "Murphy," was all he said as he turned and headed toward the elevator. Stepping into the elevator, he pushed on of the buttons. As the elevator door started to close, he looked at her and spoke. "Good luck," was all he said with a devious smile.

Max nodded to him as the elevator door closed. Turning to head toward O'Brien's office, she proceeded to unbutton her top button. Arriving at the captain's office, she knocked on the door.

"Enter," a voice from inside called out.

Max opened the door and stepped inside. "If it's good news, leave the door open, or if it's bad, get in here and close it," the man behind the huge wooden desk commanded. Max saw a small, bald headed, elderly man with a beer belly and the bluest eyes she had ever seen. He was sitting at a desk covered with files and folders but no computer or computer screen on the desk. "Who are you and what do you want?" He barked at Max. She was starting to believe she might had made a big mistake.

"I'm Detective Maxine Somers and I've been transferred here from the 34th." Max stated hesitantly.

" So you're the one McDaniel speaks so highly of. What he did failed to say was how attractive you are." He said, his whole demeanor changing almost immediately toward her.

"Thank you but I think maybe Captain McDaniel might have exaggerated a little." Max replied.

"No, I don't think so. We need more women like you in the department. Young, attractive and willing to go under cover," he explained to Max.

She started to feel panic starting to set in. Going undercover was not what she had in mind doing as a detective.

She had done some undercover work before at the 34th, and she hated every minute of it.

Trying to give the impression of being a team player, she replied. "It's an honor to be here, Sir. Since I am still a rookie detective, I'm afraid I don't have much experience with undercover work. I am willing to learn, however," she lied.

That seemed to satisfy the chief for the moment, as he started looking through the pile of folders on his desk. Finally finding the file he was looking for; he opened it and addressed her. "It says here in your jacket that you scored very well in your testing and procedure but have little or no experience, other than patrol, in the field. Is that correct?" he asked.

"Yes, it is, but I am an adaptive learner." She reassured him.

"It also says that you're in therapy for PTSD that you acquired in Afghanistan. Is that correct? You sure you got it under control? I don't want you going Rambo on me and shooting up the department," He asked tentatively.

"That won't happen, Sir," she replied, continuing, "Some times smoke in the air will trigger my symptoms but I take medication to keep it under control, and my therapy is helping a lot."

"Good, I'm sure more than half our officers here probably have PTSD in one form or another. Captain McDaniel wrote some very impressive reviews for you." The captain began reading from the folder. " Smart, collaborates well, and shows incentive. He says you're a real go-getter." After he finished reading her file, he closed it and threw it back onto the pile of other files. "Okay. I guess you're ready to get settled in," he told her, pushing a button on the intercom on his desk.

"Sir?" a voice replied through the intercom speaker.

"Get in here," O'Brien growled.

It seemed almost instantaneously that a middle aged man, dressed in a business suit, appeared in the captain's office.

"Yes Sir," the man stated, while he started looking over Max.

"This is Detective Somers," O'Brien told him. "This is her first day here. Show her where Mathew's old desk is and get her settled in. Give her the royal tour and then find Sonny. I'm pairing her up with him as her partner."

The man's eyes widened and then looking at Max, asked "You sure you want to pair her up with Sonny?"

Captain O'Brien gave him a stern look and then gruffly told him, "Get it done, now."

The man saw the look O'Brien had given him, and immediately opened the office door and hurriedly escorted Max out of the office and proceeded to showed her where her cubicle and desk was. What he didn't see was the look of panic on Max's face.

She was led by the man through a labyrinth of cubicles until they got to one that had obviously been cleaned out. The desk was bare except for a phone sitting on it and there was nothing on the walls to indicate anyone had ever been there before. The ergonomic chair showed years of wear like someone had used it for a very long time. The man proceeded to introduce himself.

"My name is Detective Forester, but everybody just calls me Frank," he started out, extending his hand in greeting. "Is everything here acceptable to you? If not, I can get whatever you need. There is a manual in the desk explaining the phone system and the most frequently used numbers," he told her as Max shook his hand back.

"Thank you. I'm Detective Maxine Somers. You can call me Max. Everything looks good, but I think the chair might be on its last leg. It will work for now but is it possible to maybe get a replacement?" She asked.

"Sure, no problem. I'll put in a request for it today. Should only take a couple of days before it's here. Will that work for you?" Frank asked, continuing, "In the meantime, you can move into here and make it yours. If you need anything else, just let me know. Here is my number." He told her, handing her his card. "By the way. I'll have new cards made up for you. As a detective you'll need them in the field. The captain insists that all the detectives carry and distribute them," Frank explained to her.

"Speaking of Captain O'Brien. Is he always so, how should I say this, abrupt?" Max asked him.

"O'Brien is an acquired taste. He'll mellow after you've been here awhile." Frank told her.

"What about my new partner, Sonny? What can you tell me about him?" Max questioned.

"Well- He's really an acquired taste. Now don't get me wrong, and I don't want to scare you off, but most of his partners don't last too long with him, but he is a good cop. He just does things his own way, and he's kind of opinionated," he explained to her. "The chief has run out of people who will work with him, so he usually assigns the rookies as his partner. They usually request a new partner within a couple of months, so the turnover is high. But I got a feeling that you'll do just fine working with him." Frank explained to her, confidently.

Max hoped he was right. Pausing to think about her options, she realized that she had made her bed, now she had to sleep in it. "So, my partner's name is Sonny. Anything else I should know about him?" Max questioned.

"Yeah! The captain is the only one who calls him Sonny. He does it to piss him off because he hates his first name. The rest of us call him by his last name," he told her.

"And what is that?" she asked hesitantly.

"Murphy," he told her.

"Murphy is my new partner?" Max exclaimed, her thoughts racing back to earlier, to the man she met at the elevator.

"Any other questions?" Frank asked.

"Just one. How come all of the detectives work on this floor and not on the third floor? At the 34th, officers and detectives work in the same department." She inquired.

"Used to be that way but when O'Brien took over, he wanted to keep the detectives close to him so he can monitor them more easily. That's why the detectives are on the same floor as him." Frank replied.

"I guess that make some sense," Max responded,

In a soft whisper, Frank told her, " No, it really doesn't."

# Chapter 3

Max had a restless night's sleep, tossing and turning most of the night, thinking at her first full day at her new job, with her new partner. She wasn't sure if she was looking forward to it, or not. Arriving at the precinct, she parked her car in the basement parking garage and rode the elevator up to the fifth floor. She had brought a small box of personal things she wanted to put on her desk and on the wall of her cubicle.

Arriving at her cubicle, she was greeted by the sight of Murphy sitting on the corner of her desk, waiting for her. A brand-new office chair was next to the desk. *Frank certainly didn't waste any time on procuring her request,* she thought to herself.

Placing her box of items on her desk she turned and spoke to her new partner. "Thanks for the heads up the other day when we first met. It helped a lot. I know you know who I am but just for the record, let me introduce myself. My name is Maxine Somers, but most people just call me Max."

"Murphy," was all he said.

"Nice to meet you, Murphy. I think we will work well together." Max stated in an up-beat manner. Trying to start off in a positive note.

"Right." Murphy replied. "Loo,I hate breaking in new partners, so just do what I tell you to do, and we'll great along fine. Got it?" he said gruffly.

"Got it." Max replied enthusiastically.

"My desk is on the other side of yours," he told her, pointing over the partition wall. "When I yell, you come running. Got it?"

"Yes Sir," she replied.

"I said my name is Murphy- not sir. Now I'll leave you to get settled in, and good luck," he told her. Turning, he left her cubicle and Max just stood there, dumbfounded.

*Well, that was interesting,* she thought as she sat down in her new office chair.

She spent the morning unpacking her personal items for her office space, a picture of her daughter on her desk. A note pad and some pens in her desk drawer and a tape dispenser and stapler on top of her desk. Frank stopped by and brought her some empty file folders and other items she would be needing. Max thanked him and commented on the speed and efficiency of getting her the new chair.

She then spent the rest of the day familiarizing herself with the phone system, only taking a break to have her lunch and a cup of coffee in the break room. She was pleasantly surprised at the quality of the coffee in the break area as the coffee at her previous workplace tasted like tar, plus there was a fully stocked vending machine with sandwiches and chips. This was good to know in case she didn't bring a lunch.

About four thirty, she heard Murphy yell at her from over the partition. "Rookie- get your weapon and a notepad and pen. We have a case."

Max quickly grabbed what gear she needed and joined Murphy at his desk.

"You ever investigated a murder scene, rookie?" Murphy asked as they headed for the elevator.

"I've covered a couple of homicides before but only as a beat cop. Never as a detective," she replied, stepping into the elevator.

"Okay then. Get ready for a baptism by fire, baby. A baptism by fire," he told her as he pushed the button for the garage. Max wanted to tell him off about how she felt about the "rookie" and the "baby" comments, but held her tongue, figuring it was neither the time nor place.

Getting into an unmarked squad car, they proceeded to the high end area of Beverly Hills. "What have we got?" Max inquired.

"Dispatch said we have three dead in north Beverly Hills. Apparently shot and found by the daughter when she got home from school. Doesn't seem to be a robbery," he told her. "When we get there, keep your mouth shut, your eyes open, and record everything I tell you to. You got it," he demanded.

"Got it." Max replied, her anger slowly seething away at her. In her head, she knew he was right to make her learn the ropes, but she still resented the way he talked to her.

Arriving at the crime scene, Max observed a half dozen police cars parked in the circular driveway of a large mansion, along with a couple of ambulances. Their lights flashing red and blue. There was also a new Corvette and an older Mustang convertible parked next to the garage area. Several officers were gathered around the Italian marble fountain, a couple of other officers were putting up crime scene tape. Two others were investigating some thing but from her angle, she couldn't see what they were processing.

"Must be money involved." Murphy stated as they pulled into the driveway.

"And lots of it." Max said out loud.

Entering the mansion, Max was amazed at the opulence of the rooms in her sight. Murphy saw her looks of amazement and whispered, "Don't let all this money make you forget this is a murder investigation, not a sightseeing tour." His comment snapped her back into the real world and the job they had come to do.

There was a uniformed officer standing by the door of the foyer. Seeing their badges, he told them, "They're out by the pool," and pointed them in the direction of the pool doors. Entering the pool area, Max saw several police officers searching around the plants and shrubs in the back yard around the pool. Laying on the cement pool deck were two bodies covered with sheets and a third person lying on an ambulance stretcher with several medical personnel gathered around the woman strapped on to it.

The medical examiner was bent over one of the two bodies with a device that looked like a large ink pen. He was waving it over the upper torso of the man's body that was partially covered under the sheet. Seeing Max, he covered the sheet back over the body.

"Hey Charlie, how's your boss?" Murphy asked the coroner, continuing, "What have we got here?"

The man with the device rose from the body. "Hi Murphy. I guess you drew the short straw," He quipped, glancing in Max's direction. Max knew what he meant.

Continuing, he stated. "Three dead and one close to it," looking at the medics wheeling out the woman on the stretcher.

"I was told three dead. What changed"" Murphy questioned.

"Well, when the first officers arrived, they thought they had three bodies. One on the deck, and two in the pool. Turned out the woman on the deck was close to expiring, but the first officers on the scene were able to administer first aid and stabilized her," the Medical Examiner told him, continuing, "She still may not make it. She's lost a lot of blood."

"Okay, that makes two dead and one critical," Murphy stated. "Where's number three?

"Out in the front fountain. They found the gardener in the pond when they searched the grounds. He was apparently shot too, but his clothing got sucked into the water intake pump, and the cops are having a hard time extracting him from the pump motor. I'm guessing he probably was the first to killed." The Medical Examiner stated.

"You keep saying apparently shot. Aren't you sure?" Murphy questioned.

"I found some gunpowder burns on the back of the wounded woman, but look what happens when I run my metal detector over the bullet entry point on the man." He then threw back the sheet off of the man and run the pen like metal detector around and stuck it into the bullet hole in his back. Nothing happened, no sound indicating any metal in the wound.

"No bullets. Got no powder burns on the man's skin or the other dead woman. Pool water probably washed it away. but they both have a bullet hole in their backs, and for the life of me, I can't find a bullet in either one of them. Our surviving woman seems to have been shot at very close range, not the same as the other victims. No bullet either, but powder burns on her skin. So apparently the man and the one woman were shot from a distance, the survivor up close and I'll bet the body in the fountain will be the same. He was probably shot up close,too," the M.E. stated, "And by the way, so far we haven't found any brass casings either."

"Not a through and through?" Murphy asked'

"Nope. The bullet went in, but nothing came out." The M.E. explained.

" Somebody doesn't want us to find any evidence," Murphy declared. "By the way, who did find them?"

"The daughter, when she got home from school." The M.E. told him.

" Lucky girl. Where is she?" Murphy questioned.

"Upstairs in her bedroom," he was told by the M.E.

Murphy proceeded to walk over to Max and told her, "Detective Somers, go find the daughter and get her statement. Write down everything she tells you, no matter how trivial."

"Will do." Max replied, taking out her notebook and ink pen and headed for the stairs off the great room. Walking up to the second floor, she spotted a uniformed officer standing in front of one of the rooms in the hallway. The door was closed. The officer saw her gold badge as she walked up to him and moved to the side of the door for her.

Max took a deep breath and then softly knocked on the door. A young girl's voice on the other side yelled at her to go away. Max heard sobbing in her voice.

"I'm Detective Somers. Can I come in and talk to you? I have some questions that need answers." Max pleaded through the door.

Silence ensued from her request. After about a minute, she heard the click of the lock as it was turned. Softly opening the door, she stepped into the bedroom. It appeared to be a typical teenage girl's room. She observed a sixteen or seventeen year old girl sitting on the bed, crying. A Kleenex box sat next to her with a waste basket almost full of used tissues.

"Are you okay?" Max asked her.

"I just found my father's body floating in the swimming pool. How do you think I am." The girls choked out between sobs.

"I'm sorry about you mother and father being shot..." Max started out.

"Mary wasn't my mother. She was my stepmother, and I'm glad she got shot." The young girl blurted out, surprising Max with her vindictiveness.

Max decided to try a different tack. "My name is Detective Maxine Somers, but you can call me Max. What is your name and how old are you?" she told her as she moved over to the edge of the bed and sat on the corner of it.

"I'm Lisa Lewis and I'm seventeen," she replied.

"Lisa, do you feel up to answering a few questions for me?" Max asked.

The girl grabbed a tissue out of the box, wiped her eyes and answered. "What do you want to know?"

Max got out her notebook and a pen. "What time did you arrive home, this afternoon?"

"I got out of school about three fifteen and arrived home around four. I walked into the house and started for my room, when I saw a bunch of sacks with clothes in them on the foyer floor, and the pool door open. My dad always complains about the air conditioning bill, so I went to close it. That's when I saw Mary lying on the deck of the pool. At first I thought she was drunk and passed out, until I saw the blood." Lisa volunteered.

Max wrote what she was told in her notebook, then asked. "What did you do next?"

"When I approached Mary on the ground, that's when I then saw my dad and Marie, our maid, floating face down in the pool. I jumped into pool and tried to pull them out of the water. I quickly realized that I was too late, so then I called 911 on my phone." Lisa explained to Max.

"Did you happen to see anybody leaving when you came home?" Max asked.

"No, I didn't see anybody when I got home." Lisa said.

"Do you know if your parents had any enemies or anyone who had a problem with them?" Max queried.

"As far as my dad, I would have to say no. Everybody loved him. As far as my stepmother, I really don't know or care," she replied to Max.

"I take it you and your stepmother didn't get along." Max stated.

Lisa didn't reply immediately, then told Max, "No I didn't. Neither did my brother," she then took another tissue and blew her nose. "Look- My father was fifty-seven, rich and divorced. She was twenty- six, broke and a gold-digger. She latched onto my father like the leach that she was, and he was so infatuated with having a new trophy wife. I'm not even sure she was faithful to him, but he indulged her every whim. The only thing she was good at was spending my dad's money and making my life utterly miserable."

Max was taken aback by Lisa's exclamation, then decided to try a different tack. "Okay then," Max paused. Trying to think of another question. "What did your dad do for a living? He must have been very successful at his work, "she inquired.

Lisa started sobbing again, took another tissue, then blurted out. "He's a gum manufacturer and distributor."

Max misunderstood what she had said, thinking she had said gun. "Your father was in the gun business?" she asked.

Lisa, through her sobs and tissues, replied curtly. "No! Gum, not gun. He imports ingredients and manufactures gum. You know, chewing gum."

"Oh, gum not gun." Max replied, scratching out what she had written in her notebook and writing in the new word. "Okay, I guess that covers just about everything I need." Then having thought of another question, asked. "You said you have a brother. Can I ask where he is?"

"Ross is in his final year of pre-med at UCLA. He lives on campus." Lisa volunteered.

"Would you know his address and phone number? Would you like us to inform him of what has happened here?" Max gently asked her.

"Oh God! He doesn't know yet," Lisa cried out, starting to cry again. "I can't tell him. I just can't talk to him yet, I just can't."

"Do you have his telephone number or his address? We can have an officer get a hold of him, if you want." Max asked.

Lisa paused for a moment or two and then replied. "Everything you need should be on a piece of paper on the refrigerator door in the kitchen." After giving the information to Max, she started crying again and buried her face on a pillow on the bed.

Max realized that Lisa was in no frame of mind to answer any more questions, so she quietly exited the room and nodded to the officer guarding the door. Going downstairs, she found the kitchen and copied down the information needed to contact the brother. Finding Murphy, she saw he was finishing up with the medical examiner, she handed him the son's contact information, telling him that he needed to make the phone call.

Murphy tried to hand the piece of paper back to Max, but she managed to avoid his attempt at passing the responsibility. "Oh no, policy says the senior officer makes the call, and that's you," she told him. Realizing that she knew the procedure, he accepted his duty by putting the paper in his pocket. Max could tell he wasn't happy about it.

"We're done here. What did you get from the girl?" Murphy asked.

"I tell you in the car. Did you get everything we needed?" Max inquired.

"Yeah, but we need more information from the medical examiner when he gets done with the bodies," he informed Max, then asked. "Now your turn. What did you get from the girl?"

Max went over the notes with him, she had taken from Lisa. Murphy paid particular attention when Max informed him that the dead man was in the gum manufacturing business. He was silent for a couple of minutes, then spoke softly. Max couldn't tell if he was talking to himself or to her.

"Three dead, one almost dead. Nothing appears to be stolen, so it's not a robbery and no bullet casings or even bullets were found. Looks like a professional hit. Business owner who manufactures gum. So, he deals in imports and exports of products. Maybe he's importing more than gum?" Speaking his thoughts out loud, then turning to Max, informed her, "We need to look into his business dealings and find out who he might have pissed off," he informed Max.

"When we get back to the office, I want you to make the arrangements to visit the victim's business. Also check the hospital on the wife's condition and find out when we can interview her, and then you can start the paperwork on the investigation" Murphy told her. Max realized that she wasn't getting home anytime soon.

"Besides informing the son, what else are you going to do," Max asked sarcastically.

"Oh yeah, I've got a date with a beer at Mike's Bar. Are you sure you won't make the call for me? I hate that part of the job," he informed her.

"Sorry, you're senior officer, so it's procedure. Besides, I got a full plate based on what you want done already," she informed him. A scowl appeared on Murphy's face and silence followed all the way to the office.

Arriving at the precinct parking garage, Max exited the squad car and headed up the elevator to her desk. As the elevator door closed, she saw Murphy start up his car and peel out of the garage on his way to the bar, leaving a trail of rubber and smoke on the concrete.

# Chapter 4

Max got home late that night after finally completing her projects that were assigned to her by Murphy. After a late supper, she lay in her bed and went over the events of the day. Her thoughts then dwelt on her working relationship with Murphy, going over the pros and cons of trying to work with him. She knew he was a real jerk, she had worked with other men just like him, both in the military and in the police department, but realized she could still learn a lot from him about being a good detective. She knew she could work with him, but didn't know how long she could tolerate him.

Finally drifting off to sleep, she awoke rested and refreshed, having not heard any late night fighting from the next door neighbors. Driving to work, she mentally steeled herself for dealing with Murphy. She knew that the two of them were going to have a royal knock down blow up fight, she just hoped it wouldn't be today. Arriving at her desk, she was surprised at a bouquet of flowers on her desk. A card was attached.

'Congratulations on surviving your first day with Murphy and taking the big one for the team, Frank,' the card read. All Max could do was smile and put the card in her desk drawer. The second thing she noticed was a brand-new computer and keyboard on her desk. Her password and username were on a post-it note, stuck on the computer screen. She proceeded to turn on the computer and put the needed identification information into it for sign on.

She spent a few minutes engrossed in exploring the forms and mail capabilities of the new computer when she was interrupted by Murphy coming up behind her. He had a small box in his hand. He threw it onto her desk and said, "You're going to need these," he informed her. She opened the box and found it contained her contact business cards.

"Thank you for getting these for me." Max exclaimed as she took some of the cards out of the box and placed them in her pocket.

"No problem, rookie. Did you get us an appointment in to our victim's gum business?" Murphy asked curtly.

"Yes, we are all set for our visit after lunch." Max informed him.

"Good! First we got a date with the medical examiner and also with our survivor's doctor at the hospital, hopefully for an update." Murphy informed her. Throwing her the keys to the squad car, he added. "You're driving."

Max felt relief because Murphy looked like he had been on an all-night bender. From the way he looked, she couldn't be sure if he wasn't still drunk.

"Okay," she replied. The two of them proceeded down to the parking garage. As Max was getting into their car, she noticed that Murphy was nowhere to be seen. Then she heard what sounded like him throwing up his guts behind a concrete support pillar. When he returned to the car, Max asked him, "Are you okay?" with genuine concern in her voice.

"Yeah," he replied. "I think I might have had some bad buffalo wings last night."

Max thought of a couple comments she could have made but decided to keep them to herself.

Murphy gave her the address to the county medical examiner's office as Max started the car. As they pulled out of the dimly lit garage into the bright California sun, it caused Max to squint her eyes for a moment to adjust to the brightness. Coming up to a stoplight, she looked over and saw Murphy sound asleep, his head on the side window, the sun full force on his sweating face. *Bad buffalo wing, my ass,* she thought to herself as she accelerated away from the stop light. Murphy didn't move as he gently snored away.

Arriving at the building that housed the medical examiner's office, Max parked the car in the available space in front of the building, designated for police parking. Murphy had slept the entire twenty minutes it took to get there.

"Hey Murphy, wake up. Looks like we're here," she spoke loudly, almost yelling at him.

Murphy's eyes slowly opened. He stretched himself in the car seat, yawned and then asked,

"Are we here already?" as he energetically jumped out of the car and started heading toward the building.

Max followed behind, letting Murphy take the lead since she wasn't sure where to go, it being her first time there. Murphy led her through the front door and into the elevator. He pushed the button for the basement. As the doors started to close, he asked Max, "You don't have a queasy stomach, do you?"

"No, I don't, but you're looking a little pale," she told Murphy with a smile. "Are you sure you're, okay?"

Murphy gave her a disdainful look and replied, "I'm fine. Just don't go spilling your guts out all over the floor. Doc will make you clean up your own mess. I've seen some real macho dudes lose their stomachs here before, so I just wanted to warn you."

"Consider me warned." Max told him. Just as she said that, the elevator stopped, and the doors opened. The stench that filled the elevator was almost overpowering. Murphy looked at Max with a grin and stepped out of the elevator. Max continued to follow him as they went down a corridor passing a half a dozen corpses laying on gurneys parked on one side of the wall. They were all covered in sheets, but you could tell from the smell that some of them were in an advanced state of decomposition. A couple of them even had maggots crawling on the sheet and dropping onto the floor. Max tried to avoid the sight and the stench as she followed Murphy down the corridor, looking straight ahead.

Reaching a door at the end of the corridor, Murphy stopped before opening it and told Max, "Get ready for Hell, and don't show any weakness or Doctor Death will stick it to you hard."

Max had no idea what to expect as Murphy opened the door and held it open for her to go in first. Once inside Max felt like she was dropped into Dante's Inferno. There were four autopsy tables with a gowned and masked man at each one, all in different stages of autopsies procedures. One was eviscerating bowels from a dead woman; another was in the process of removing the top of a man's skull. Yet a third man was stitching up another man with the classic Y shaped chest incision. She recognized him as the medical examiner from their crime scene. The fourth man looked up from a corpse he was in the process of making a chest incision. Then seeing them, stopped. "Murphy- good to see you again. Is this your new partner?" He asked as he put down his scalpel and walked over to them.

"Yup, this is Detective Maxine Somers and we're assigned to the Lewis case." Murphy told him, continuing, "Max, this is Doctor Deitrich, our chief medical examiner."

The doctor walked over to Max, removed his latex gloves, throwing them in an overflowing trash can, and shook her hand. Max felt that his hands were ice cold.

"Doctor Emil Deitrich at your service," he told her as he took her hand. Max heard a heavy German accent and an air of culture and sophistication in his voice. "Can I give your beautiful partner a tour of our facilities, Murphy?" he asked, still holding Max's hand.

"No- afraid there's no time for that today. We got to get going on our triple homicide. The boss wants this cleaned up quickly. What have you got for us?" Murphy requested.

"Such a shame. It's not often we get a beautiful woman down here. At least the ones that are still alive. Perhaps another time." he told her. Then kissing Max's hand, released it and walked over to his desk. Pulling several files from the file separator, he opened them and told them, "Strange, very strange," he started out. "The Hispanic man, I assume the gardener, was shot from a short distance once in the stomach but died from drowning. Bruising shows that someone held him underwater in a fishpond until he was dead after shooting him. The man and the women that were found in the pool were shot in he back at a long-range distance, fifteen, maybe twenty feet, leaving no powder burns on the back of their bodies. They were dead before they went into the water. But in all three cases, there were no bullets found in the wounds.

The entry holes were equivalent to a forty-five-caliber weapon but absolutely no bullets were found and no evidence of extraction, and none of the wounds were through and through. The bullets went in but they never came out. They just disapeared. Very strange, very strange indeed." He concluded.

"Any ideas?" Murphy asked.

"Well at first, I thought a pneumatic nail gun might have been used and then the nail extracted. The problem with that is you need a compressor and hose to fire that type of gun. Not very portable or convenient to use. The second problem is the wound size. A nail is much smaller than the hole it made. The second problem is the gun powder residue. Air powered nail guns don't leave gun powder residue.

My second thought was a twenty-two-caliper nail driver that they use for shooting construction nails into concrete. That would leave gun powder residue but it would shoot a nail clean through a body, and you don't have that. Besides that, they are big and heavy and not very accurate, and again, create too small a hole. So, I have to say that your weapon is yet to be determined," he concluded, closing the file folder and putting it back on the desk.

Murphy and Max just stood there with nothing to say. With their silence, Deitrich continued. "So, the problem is you have three dead bodies with gunshot wounds, with no weapon or bullets that can be identified. Three dead, a gardener, a maid, and a homeowner with no motive and nothing in common except they were all at the house at the same time. That's all I can put down on my autopsy report," he concluded. Silence followed Deitrich's statement.

Murphy was the first to respond. "We have the wife in ICU at the hospital. We're hoping to get more answers from her when she's finally able to speak."

"Let me know if she had a bullet or bullet fragments in her wound, will you." Deitrich requested from them.

"Will do," Murphy replied, "And let me know if you get any more information for us." He then turned to go, with Max following, but Deitrich took Max's hand in his before she got far and said, "I see no wedding ring, so I assume you are not married. Perhaps I could interest you in a drink and dinner sometime soon, my dear. My lady friends tell me I am most charming and I would like to show you how charming I can be. May I call upon you sometime and arrange a rendezvous?" he politely asked, again kissing her hand.

Max was a little dumb founded at first, then replied, "Certainly, just so long as you don't talk about your work. Would you like my number?" Max felt it wouldn't hurt to culture new friends such as the doctor, in her new job.

"Thank you but I can get your number from personnel. Remember, we both work for the city," he replied, kissing her hand again, then releasing it. Max slightly blushed from his attention.

"You'll hear from me soon," he told her as he held the door open for her and Murphy to exit.

Once they were out of the autopsy room, they silently walked down the corridor of the dead until they got outside. Then Murphy just exploded. "What the Hell just went on back there?" he shouted. "Don't you even consider going out with Doctor Death. Not a very good idea."

"Why not, and who do you think you are to tell me who I can or can't go out with? The last time I checked, you were my partner, not my father. So don't think for a minute that you or anybody else has any thing to say in what I do or don't do during my personal time. If I still wanted to be manipulated and controlled, then I'd go back to my ex-husband. Got it?" she replied in a firm voice.

Murphy was taken aback by Max's response, said nothing and got into the squad car. Once he was inside, he barked at her, "Let's go." Max got in on the driver's side of the car and asked, "Where to?"

"The hospital," was all he said, coolly. Max started the car and proceeded to drive to the hospital and Mary Lewis.

The trip to the hospital was in dead silence. Max was busy, focusing on driving in Los Angeles traffic and Murphy sat in silence, pouting at the dressing down Max had given him earlier. Arriving at the hospital, they went to the front desk, showed their ID's and were informed which floor Mary Lewis' room was.

On the ride up in the elevator there was complete silence between them as there were several other people riding along with them. Once reaching the designated floor, they exited the elevator and proceeded down the hallway, Murphy glanced on both sides of the hallway until he found what he was looking for, an empty room.

Going into the room, he indicated to Max to follow. Once they were both in the room, Murphy closed the door then proceeded to get into Max's face. "Don't you ever talk like that to me again, ever," he told her in a forced whisper, his face turning red only a few inches from Max's.

"Don't you ever try to control me or my private life again, mister. I'll go wherever I want and see whom ever I want in my personal life. If it doesn't affect our case, you have nothing to say to me about it. Got it?" Max responded, poking him on his chest in emphasis. Her voice rising louder, the madder she became.

Suddenly the door to the room burst opened and a nurse stormed in and angrily said, "Who the hell are you people? And what are you doing in this room?" Seeing their badges didn't slow her down, "I don't know what your problems are but take them outside this hospital, or get couples counseling. We have sick people in this hospital and they don't need to hear this crap coming from you two. What are you two even doing in here?"

Max quickly explained that they were police detectives and were there to interview Mary Lewis' doctor.

"Then get out of this room and get down to the nurse's station, and try to remember where you are," she stated, chastising them both.

They both knew that she was right and left the room in silence. Once out in the hallway they both walked down to the nurse's station without looking at each other. Arriving at the station, Murphy asked for Mary Lewis' doctor. They were informed that he was in with her at the moment and that they could take a chair in the waiting area for him to come out, and that she would notify the doctor when he came out of Mary Lewis' room. They both took chairs on the opposite sides of the waiting room.

It was twenty minutes later when a doctor came in and asked if they were the ones waiting for him. Both Max and

Murphy rose and joined him. Murphy started the conversation. "Yeah, we are the investigators on the shooting of Mary Lewis," he stated, showing his badge to the doctor. Max did the same. "What can you tell us."

The doctor looked at them both and explained. "Mrs. Lewis is a very lucky woman." He started. "She was wounded in the back of the neck, A projectile entered her spinal column at approximately her third vertebrae, barely missing her spinal cord. She had a massive amount of blood loss, so is still touch and go as far as her survival. But for now, we have her stabilized and in recovery."

"Any chance we can talk to her any time soon?" Murphy asked.

"Not for a while," the doctor replied. "It's going to take a day or two before we are sure she is out of danger."

"Did you recover the bullet from the wound?" Max asked. "The medical examiner couldn't find a bullet in any of the wounds of the other victims. We were hoping you might have been luckier," Max inquired.

"No- no bullet wound if that's what it was. All we found was a large hole in the back of her neck. No bullet but lots of trauma." The doctor responded.

"Did you bag and tag her clothes she had on when she came in?" Murphy asked.

"Of course, we did. Check with the nurse at the station and she will retrieve them for you. Anything else you need?" he asked them.

"No, that should about do it for now. If there are any changes, could you give us a call?" Murphy requested.

"Certainly- do you have a card?" the doctor asked.

"My partner will give you one." Murphy replied, signaling Max to give him one of hers, as he abruptly left the room and headed to the nurse's station, leaving Max to give the doctor her card.

Joining Murphy at the nurse's station, she whispered, "Thanks partner." With sarcastic emphasis on the word 'Partner.'

Murphy didn't respond to her dig, but just ignored her comment until a nurse handed them a sealed plastic bag containing Mary Lewis' clothing and personal effects.

"Sign for the evidence and sign and date the bag, partner," he told Max as he walked away from the station. Max followed the procedure and signed the release document and then signed the evidence with her signature and time and date on the red seal of the bag.

Taking the evidence bag and heading down the hallway, she saw Murphy standing in the elevator. Thinking he was holding it open for her, she sped up her pace. Just as she was twenty feet from the elevator, he gave her a grin and let the elevator door close on her, waving at her as the door slowly closed, knowing she couldn't get to it in time.

*God- what an ass.* She thought to herself, but she was determined she wasn't going to let him get to her. She pushed the elevator button and waited for the elevator to return. When it did, she went down to the main floor and then out to where the car was parked. Sitting in the car was Murphy, smoking a cigarette, a grin on his face.

"Surprised you even waited here for me," Max told him.

"Had to, you got the keys. Can we go now, partner." Using the same sarcasm that she had used on him earlier.

"Gladly," she replied, as she started the car and headed back to the precinct in silence.

Arriving back at the precinct, Max got out of the squad car and took the elevator to the evidence floor. Signing in the evidence bag, she then headed up to her cubicle and took her lunch to the squad break room. Murphy didn't follow her there, and she was very thankful for that.

Frank was in the break room having his lunch when she came in. Seeing Max, he signaled for her to come and join him. Happy to see a familiar face, she came over to his table and pulled up a chair.

"Glad to see a friendly face," she told Frank.

"Rough morning?" Frank asked.

"You don't know the half of it," she replied.

"Murphy?" Frank questioned.

"You really don't know the half of it," she repeated again with a heavy sigh.

"By the way, did you get the business cards I had made for you? Murphy picked them up this morning from me and said he would get them to you." He told her.

Max just hung her head in resignation knowing that Murphy had lied to her, telling her that he had them made. "Thanks Frank. I really appreciate everything you've done for me." She told him sincerely.

"No problem, just glad I can help you out," he replied. "What's on your agenda for the afternoon?"

"Going to our victim's workplace. He was an importer and manufacturer of chewing gum products. I hope that maybe we can find a link between his work and his death." Max explained to him.

"You're thinking drugs?" Frank asked.

"Make sense, doesn't? His company has the importing capabilities and a distribution network. It could be the perfect way to camouflage a drug operation. Perhaps a competitor made a move to take over the operation," she told Frank.

"Your idea or Murphy's?" Frank questioned.

"Actually mine, but Murphy probably will take credit for it if it pans out," she jokingly told him.

"You're probably right about that," he agreed, continuing, "just remember the first rule of detective work, you have to..."

"Follow the money," Max finished his sentence for him.

"Right- follow the money," Frank repeated.

As they finished their break, several other officers entered the break room and started eating their lunches. There was a steady buzz of background noise from the officer's conversation when suddenly the room was dead silent. Frank was facing the doorway and whispered a warning to Max, "Murphy's here."

As Murphy walked through the break room, he acknowledged several of the officers in the room. Their response back to him were cool but polite. Max prayed he wouldn't say something to embarrass her. Her prayer wasn't answered.

Walking over to the table where Max and Frank were sitting, he spoke in a loud enough voice to be heard by everybody in the room, "Hey rookie, breaks over. We got a gum manufacturing business to visit. Can't solve any crimes sitting on your butt in here."

Max felt her face blush from his comment. Frank saw her reaction and started to raise from his chair to rise to her defense but was stopped when Max put her hand on his arm and shook her head. "I got this," she whispered to Frank. Then in an equally as loud a voice as Murphy's, said, "Yup, you're right. I wasn't sure if you were going to be up for the afternoon. Looks like you're feeling better after those bad buffalo wings last night," her voice dripping in sarcasm.

There were snickers from some of the officers in the break room upon Max's comment. They knew that Murphy's illness was anything but bad buffalo wings. Murphy heard the snickers from the fellow officers and decided it was in his best interest not to escalate.

"Okay. Whenever you are ready to go, I'll be waiting for you by the elevator." Murphy stated, slightly humbled.

"Fine- I'll meet you there when I'm done here," she told him.

After Murphy exited the break room, Frank started clapping his hands. Most of the other officers then followed suit. "I've never seen anybody stand up to Murphy like that before," he exclaimed. "In my ten years on the force, you're the first person to really stand up to him. You must be one mean mother," he gushed.

"Damn straight," Max replied with a grin. "And don't you forget it." Then touching the hand of Frank, she told him with a grin, "Don't worry, you're safe."

*Thank God for small favors*, Frank thought to himself as Max left the break room to join Murphy.

*That felt so good,* Max thought to herself as she headed for the elevator.

# Chapter 5

The drive to the factory was made in total silence. Murphy rode in a sullen mood, licking his wounds from the verbal altercation in the break room, and Max knew that Murphy was pouting but didn't want to feed any more fuel to the fire.

Pulling up in front of the gum company, she was amazed at the modern building and office complex the business entailed. She could see from Murphy's expression that he was impressed too.

"This isn't what I was expecting," Max informed Murphy.

"Me either. Really doesn't look like a drug business," he replied, continuing, "But, sometimes looks can be deceiving," he added.

"Let's find someone to talk to," Max countered, trying to lighten the mood between them.

They both began walking into the main building that appeared to be the headquarters and offices. Once inside they saw a huge open atrium and reception desk located in the middle of the room. Approaching the desk, the receptionist acknowledged them and asked how she could help direct them.

Murphy identified themselves as police detectives and asked to talk to someone in charge of operations. The receptionist immediately got on her headset. Max could hear her talking to someone on the other end. When the conversation on the headset was over, the receptionist informed them that a company spokesperson would be down shortly. As they waited, sitting on expensive leather chairs in the atrium, Max told Murphy, " Obviously we're dealing with big money here, so take it easy on the interrogation. Remember you catch more flies with honey than vinegar." Murphy just scowled at her. A few minutes later a tall, tan, statuesque, attractive, thirty something woman exited the elevator and walked up to them. Max immediately hated her, but Murphy looked like he was in love.

"Good afternoon, officers. My name is Francine Jackson and I'm the CFO for Lewis Industries. How may I help you?" she said with a smile that displayed her perfect, brilliantly white teeth.

Max and Murphy showed their badges, then Murphy began by asking if they could go somewhere more private and talk about a sensitive matter.

"Certainly officers, please follow me," she responded. She then escorted them to the elevator. Rising to the top floor, she led them to her office and bid them to take a seat in the chairs in front of her desk. Once everybody was seated, she asked, "What can I do for you?"

Murphy started. "First of all, I want to express our condolences about the death of Mr. Lewis."

"Thank you. It was a great loss for me personally and to the whole company at large. He will be greatly missed here and, in the community," she responded. Max thought she saw tears welling up in her eyes.

Murphy then asked his next question. "Did Mr. Lewis have any problems with anyone here at work or anybody else who might have a grudge against him?"

Ms. Jackson thought for a couple of moments, then spoke. "I can't be sure about outside of work, but here, he had absolutely no problems with anybody. In fact, since his company went public on the stock market, he hardly spent much time here at all. He spent most of his time with his new wife and his son and daughter. I truly think that after the divorce, for the first time in a long time, he was truly enjoying his life."

Max then asked, "There's an ex-wife? Perhaps she held a grudge against him."

Ms. Jackson then told them, in almost a whisper, "Yes, there is an ex-wife, but he has been divorced from her for several years."

"Perhaps she was upset about the divorce and decided to do something to get back at him," Murphy questioned.

Ms. Jackson shook her head negatively and informed them, again in almost a whisper, "I don't know how that could be. She's been in an institution for almost five years. Mr. Lewis had her institutionalized when she became psychotic and tried to kill herself, her husband and the daughter in a suicide attempt."

Murphy was taken aback by the information for a moment or two, then asked. "Any chance she might have got out or escaped?"

"I doubt it. Mr. Lewis just visited her a week or two ago. He said that she was so drugged that she didn't even recognize him," she explained.. That answer seemed to satisfy Murphy but sparked Max's attention.

"If Mr. Lewis wasn't here much lately, how come you know so much about his visit to his ex-wife?" Max questioned.

Ms. Jackson immediately turned red. Max knew exactly what that blush meant. "You were having an affair with him, weren't you?" Max asked.

Ms. Jackson deflated emotionally like a punctured balloon, before them and began to gently cry. It took a while before she had composed herself before she could answer. "Yes." Was all she said.

Murphy, seeing an opportunity to interject, stated, "Is that why you killed him? Because he married someone else."

"Oh, God no!" she blurted out. "I loved him too much to hurt him."

"Do you have an alibi for yesterday afternoon, when he was killed?" Murphy demanded. Max tried to signal him to tone his attitude down.

"Yes- I was here at work all day preparing a quarterly report," she countered. "There must be a dozen people here that can verify that. Check with Russell Peters, our operations manager. He was with me most of the day in conferences. He'll verify I was here all day and well into the evening."

"We'll do that. Speaking of operations, it seems that this business would be a good front for importing certain illegal merchandise and distributing it elsewhere. You wouldn't know anything about that would you?" Murphy questioned her aggressively.

Max felt her stomach start to churn because of Murphy's abrasive attitude and tone of voice in his questioning of Ms. Jackson. Jumping in, she tried to make Murphy's question less intrusive. "What my partner means is, that Mr. Lewis seems to have been assassinated by persons unknown. We were thinking that drugs might be involved, and that it possibly was a drug hit from someone also in the business. There wouldn't be any validity in that assumption is there?" Max rephrased the question.

Ms. Jackson sat at her desk in apparently stunned silence. The enormity of the implications of the question seemed to cause her to be at a loss for words. Finally, she had the presence of mind to reply. "Drugs? Oh God no!" She exclaimed. "Henry hated even taking aspirin. The thought of him being involved in drugs is the most ludicrous thing I have ever heard of."

"Why is that?" Max inquired.

"To think that someone- anyone, in this company, jeopardizing their job or their profit sharing for drug distribution, is just insane. Go ahead and check through the accounts, search our productions, because we make more millions from our gum manufacturing than we possibly ever could by selling drugs. Our records are an open book, and you're welcome to examine them," she explained to them.

"You're kidding. You're telling me selling gum is a multi-million-dollar industry? Gum?" Murphy asked incredibly.

"Yes, gum," Ms. Peterson replied continuing, "Our last financial statement showed sales of over a quarter billion dollars world wide."

Her last statement shut Murphy up.

Continuing, she informed them, "Look- Lewis Industries is a multi million-dollar import, manufacturing, and distribution company. We are on the New York Stock Exchange and doing very well as far as our commodities and sales." Pausing to think what else to say, then continuing. "With the death of Henry, not much in the company will change. The current Mrs. Lewis will take over the company, and if she doesn't want too or can't, then control will go to a conservator ship for his adult son and minor daughter. Then he and his sister will assume full control when she turns twenty-one."

"Who's the conservator?" Max asked.

Without hesitation. Ms. Jackson replied. "I am. As well as being CFO for the company, I was also Mr. Lewis' attorney."

Murphy, as Max anticipated and feared, engaged his mouth before his brain and said, "Well- Well, CFO, attorney and whore. What else were you doing for the company?"

This statement shocked Max and infuriated Ms. Jackson. Max could tell she was greatly offended as her whole demeanor changed, becoming rigid and cold. "If you have no other questions for me, I am asking you to leave the premises now." She told them with ice in her voice.

Max, realizing that Murphy had crossed the line and they wouldn't be getting any more information from her, told Ms. Jackson they were grateful for her cooperation and thanked her for her time.

"You are more than welcome back, officer," indicating Max, but your cretin of a partner is not. In fact, if he comes here again, I won't hesitate to have security haul his butt out of here, and I will make sure his supervisor gets a complaint about his foul mouth," she informed them, as she looked directly at Murphy. "Now, if there are no more questions, I have work to do." With that statement, Max realized that the interview was over. Handing her a card, she told Ms. Jackson,

"If you think of anything else that might be important, please call me at the number on my card. And again, thank you for all your time and help."

With that statement, Max exited the office with Murphy following behind her. Everything was silent between them until they exited the elevator to the ground floor. Immediately Murphy started the conversation. "I think she's hiding something. She knows more than she's admitting."

"What? Like she knows she doesn't like being insulted. I think she made that very clear. What is wrong with you, Murphy? Are you drunk? I swear you have no impulse control, no filters. You just can't talk to people like that. You're going to get into really big trouble someday," Max instructed him.

"Nah, that's never going to happen. Women like her don't bother making trouble for men like me." Murphy told her with an air of self confidence.

"Men like you. What do you mean, men like you?" Max asked, regretting the question almost immediately.

"You know, strong, self- assured and confident, and may I say, handsome as hell," he listed confidently to her with a straight face.

Max almost choked when she heard the list. She couldn't imagine where Murphy ever got the impression or the hubris to feel that his list was an accurate description of himself. She felt like she should cut him down a peg or two but decided to only make one comment. "And you have a disproportionate propensity for bad buffalo wings." This reply seemed to knock the wind out of Murphy, and he went suddenly silent.

They proceeded to the squad car and headed back to the precinct. Arriving at the squad room, they saw Frank approach them at the elevator door. "How was the afternoon? He asked both of them as they stepped off the elevator. Max replied first. "Interesting and informative." All Murphy commented was, "What she said." The tension between Max and Murphy was palatable.

Frank just smiled at Max then addressed Murphy, "Captain O'Brien wants to see you immediately, Murphy."

"I got a couple of things to do, then I'll pop in on him." Murphy casually told Frank.

"He said as soon as you arrived, and I don't think he was in a very happy mood about something." Frank reiterated, a firmness in his voice.

Murphy knew better than to ignore a direct command from his superior, so he headed to O'Brien's office but not before whispering "Bootlicker," toward Frank. He then put on an air of bravado confidence as he headed towards O'Brien's office.

"What's happening?" she asked Frank, as she watched Murphy walk away.

"He must have pissed off the wrong person today." Was all Frank had to say, with a smile on his face.

Later on, Max was sitting in her cubicle as Frank came by with a big grin on his face. Stopping at her desk, he informed her that O'Brien wanted to see her in his office. "Am I in trouble?" she asked.

"Nope." Was his reply. "Just be careful because something or some one put him in a very bad mood." As he pointed clandestinely toward Murphy's desk.

Max immediately headed toward Captain O'Brien's office. Arriving, he signaled for Max to enter. Walking in, she could see his ire on his face. "You wanted to see me, Captain?" Max asked.

"Yes I do. I want to inform you that you're on your own for three days. Your partner just earned himself a three-day vacation," he growled at her, continuing, "Were you there when he called a witness a whore?"

"Yes sir, I was." Max told him honestly.

"Okay, I just wanted to verify that for my report. I'm relying on you to continue following up on this case by yourself. Are you sure you're comfortable with that? I can assign another officer to work with you, if needed," he asked her.

"I don't think that will be necessary, but could I ask a question?" Max requested. O'Brien nodded his head in affirmation.

"I tried to warn Murphy about crossing the line during in his interrogations. I just wanted to know for sure if the complaint came from a Ms. Jackson at Lewis Manufacturing," she asked tentatively.

"Yes, it did, and the only reason you're not getting three days off too, is that she highly complemented you on your professionalism. So, keep up the good work, Detective. I'm wondering, is there any chance you possibly might wrap this case up in a few days?" he asked her.

"I don't know. The evidence is pretty sketchy. I think it will take some time and luck to solve this one. Hopefully I might get a break if our surviving witness can identify who shot her" Max truthfully told him.

"Okay, do your best to wrap it up as quick as possible. I'm giving you a deadline of a week to get some answers on this case. Got it? I want it off the books for my end of the month report," he instructed her.

"Got it." Max replied confidently. Leaving O'Brien's office, Max started second guessing if she had made the right decision about becoming a detective. Walking back to her cubicle, she was resolved to solve the case, with or without Murphy. Frank was waiting for her when she arrived. "How did it go?" he inquired.

"He gave me a week to wrap up a triple homicide, with no weapon, no suspects, and no motive. And I'm not sure where to begin," she explained to him.

Frank was silent for a moment, then replied. " Again, remember the first rule of an investigation, follow the money." Max nodded in affirmation, and then commented. "There's a lot of money involved, but what's puzzling is the main beneficiary is also a victim. The only other possibility is that the ex-wife, who has been in a mental institution for over five years."

"Tell you what. Let me buy you dinner and we can discuss the case over a glass of wine," Frank suggested

"Sounds great, but I'm afraid I don't drink alcohol, but I will accept your offer on dinner, though, if it's still okay with you," she countered.

"Fantastic. Can I pick you up around seven?" he asked.

"How about this? I'm going to be working on this case for a while. How about we leave from here, when I'm done?" she countered.

"Sounds good. I have some work I can finish up too. Let me know when you're ready," Frank answer back.

" Will do," Max replied. With dinner arranged, Max headed to her cubicle and got out her note book. Max started going through her notes she had taken throughout the investigative interviews. Nothing really popped out at her so she thought perhaps Murphy's notes might contain something to help her in the investigation.

Protocol dictated that the notes from a case never leave the police department if the investigator was not in possession of them, so Max hoped that there was a chance that Murphy had left the notebook in his desk. Walking over to his cubicle, she pulled out the center drawer of his desk. Not finding it there, she opened the side file drawer. The first thing she saw was a pint size, half full bottle of rye whiskey and a plastic glass. This didn't surprise Max, but what did catch her attention was a framed photo of Murphy, with an attractive woman, and a small boy taken in an outdoor setting by a lake.

*I didn't know that he was married and had a child. I wonder why he doesn't have the picture on top of his desk?* She thought to herself. Right next to the photo was what she was looking for, Murphy's case notebook. Taking it out of the drawer, she sat down at the desk and started going through it to see what he had written. After going through several pages, she realized what was missing.

"Son of a Bit....." she said out loud, catching herself from finishing the sentence, knowing there were still other officers working late in the room. She hoped nobody caught her outburst. Looking around, she thought nobody had heard her, until Frank came over to her cubicle.

"Everything alright?" he asked.

"You heard?" she asked.

"Me and just about everybody in the room," he told her with a grin on his face.

Max began to turn red in the face from embarrassment. "Sorry," was all she could think to say.

"Forget it, Everybody here has heard and said much worse. What did Murphy do now?" Frank asked her.

"It's what he didn't do. He told me he was going to contact the son of our victim, Henry Lewis, to inform him of the death of his father, and see if he had an alibi so we could clear him from our suspect list. I asked him to do this one thing, one little thing, but did he do it? No. He was in too much of a hurry to get to a bar, that he couldn't do just one simple thing and follow protocol. Damn, that man infuriates me." she blurted out to Frank. "How does that idiot manage to keep his badge?" she questioned angrily.

All Frank could do was stand there and listen to her verbal assault of Murphy, with a slight grin on his face. "You're not the first one to ask that same question. You have no idea how many suspensions Murphy has had." he said, trying to console Max. "I think you are in need of a good meal. This can wait until tomorrow," he told her, taking Murphy's notebook out of her hand and tossing it back into the open desk door. Seeing the notebook land next to the bottle of rye whiskey, he commented. " That doesn't surprise me one bit. It really doesn't," he explained to Max. "Lets go get something to eat. You got to be starving."

Max had to agree.

# Chapter 6

Max slowly awoke to her alarm going off. Finally fully awake, she began to reminisce about the past evening. Frank was entertaining, witty, charming, and very gay. He told her that last bit of news as they were finishing dinner at a restaurant. Max wasn't too surprised at his announcement because she had a suspicion he was, based upon the conversations they had previously at the precinct. It didn't bother Max, as she thought of him as a friend, and she needed all the friends she could get at her new job.

Just as she was getting ready to leave for work, there was a frantic knocking at the door of her apartment. Answering the door, there was a young woman, about twenty five, dressed in jeans and a tee shirt, standing there.

"Yes, can I help you?" Max asked her. Max could tell she had been crying. Several bruises on her face were in the process of turning from a deep purple to reddish pink. Max wondered how many other bruises were on her body that she couldn't see.

"I'm Pam Harris, your next door neighbor, and I apologize for interrupting you but I wanted to catch you before you left for work," the woman told her.

"I recognize your voice," Max replied, with a reassuring smile.

The woman became a little hesitant with Max's reply, saying she was sorry for all the noise she had caused.

"What can I do for you?" Max asked.

"I know we have talked before a couple of times but I was told by the building superintendent that you were a police officer. Is that true?" she asked.

"Yes." Max replied.

"Look, I really need your help. My boyfriend didn't come home from work last night, and I'm afraid something bad has happened to him. Can you help me? I don't know what I should do?" she pleaded to Max.

"Did you guys have a fight or something," Max asked, immediately regretting the question.

"No more than usual," the girl responded sheepishly.

"Well, if he is missing, you have to wait three days before you can report it to the police," Max explained.

"I understand that, it's just that Sammy runs with some rough people, and I'm afraid he might have got caught up in something he can't get out of. Could you check and see if he might have been arrested for something, please," she begged.

Max felt she didn't have time to check up on her boyfriend but then remembered her second husband using her for a punching bag, and felt pity for her. "Sure, I can check at work if he's been arrested. What's his full name?" she asked.

"Sammy, Sammy O'Brien." she told Max.

Max was struck by the similarity of her boyfriend's last name and the last name of her captain. It just seemed too strange to be a coincidence.

"He would have a father that's a police captain, would he?" Max asked, not believing that this was a coincidence.

"I doubt it, but he never talks about his family, just his hoodlum friends," the girl explained.

"Look, I'll do some asking around at the station, and see if he's been arrested. But I can't make any promises. Okay?" Max told her.

The girl immediately started to cry, taking Max's hand and thanking her. "He's really a good person, it's just that he has a lot of issues," she explained to Max.

After Max reassured her, the woman went back to her next door apartment and Max headed to work.

Arriving at work, she felt very relieved that she wasn't dealing with Murphy for three days. It almost seemed like a vacation to her. Heading to her cubicle, she knew the first thing she had to do was contact Ross Lewis. She did a computer search online and found information on him. He was twenty three, in medical school and living off campus at UCLA.

Obtaining his telephone number from her notes, she realized that if he was anything like her daughter at Berkeley, he wouldn't be available to contact until lunch time. She decided to use her personal phone and sent him a text message for him to call her when he had time. While she was thinking about it, she also sent a message to her daughter, hoping to maybe she could arrange to have a weekend with her sometime in the near future. She knew it was more than a six hour drive from Beverly Hills to Berkeley, but she knew hat she had some vacation time due to her, and she hadn't seen Alex for some time.

After sending her phone messages, she took the elevator down to the fourth floor. That was the floor for booking and holding cells, so any one arrested within the last eighteen to twenty four hours would be housed on this floor in holding cells before they were transported to central booking for arraignment.

Walking up to the intake desk, she knew she had to identify herself to the sergeant at the desk. He was a huge, muscular man, who looked like he was used to conflict, and didn't take crap from anyone. It looked to Max that he had a permanent scowl on his face, with a bad attitude to match. He was engaged in reading a newspaper.

"Good morning, sergeant. My name is Detective Somers and I'm new to this precinct." Max stated with an upbeat tone of voice. But before she could get any farther, the sergeant gruffly spoke without looking up from the newspaper he was reading, "ID," was all he said.

Max held up her ID with her shield attached, so he could see it. He looked up for a second and then barked out, "What?"

Max always believed you got more result with a smile than with a frown, so she turned on the best smile she could muster and asked, "I'm doing a favor for a friend who is afraid her boy friend might have been arrested and brought in last night. I wonder if you could possibly verify or not, whether he was arrested last night?"

The sergeant didn't even bother looking up, but asked, "Name?"

"Sammy O'Brien," she told him.

Immediately, he said, "Got no one here by that name, but we do have a John Doe brought in who had no ID on him, and refused to give his name. We're waiting for his fingerprints to come back."

"Would it be possible to see the John Doe?" she asked.

"Sure," he replied grumpily. "Sign in," he told her. Handing her a clip board with a form, providing space on it for her name, badge number, date and time. Filling out the required information on the clipboard, she handed it back to the booking sergeant,. He took it from her, looked it over then said. "Your John Doe is in cell seven. Down the aisle and to your left. It's marked. Don't forget to sign out when you're done."

"Thank you," she told him as she started down the corridor, looking for cell seven. She didn't notice the slight smile on the booking sergeant's face as he watched her as she walked way.

As she did the walk towards cell seven, she was greeted with a barrage of cat calls and obscene comments from some of the prisoners being held in the other cells. Arriving at cell seven, she saw a rough, unshaven man in his mid-twenties, sitting on the bunk. " You're Sammy O'Brien?" she told him.

"Nope. You got the wrong person." he replied. As soon as he spoke, she recognized it as the voice from the other side of her apartment wall. Max immediately knew she had the right man from her attempt at mediating between him and Pam.

"No, I got the right person. I recognize your face and voice, even though it's not through my bedroom wall." she told him.

With that statement, the man in the cell grew quiet for a moment. "You're the cop next door, aren't you. I guess Pam sent you, didn't she?"

"Yup, and believe me, I don't know why she cares, but she's very worried about you. That was a real working over you gave her recently. If it were up to me, I'd let you rot in here." Max told him disdainfully.

"I know, I know, I was wrong, but some times I just get depressed, start drinking, and take my frustrations out on her. I don't know why, but I just do it. I guess I have issues," he tried to explain to her meekly.

"Pam says the same thing about you and your issues. Look, I'll tell her I found you, but I'm not sure if she can help you. What did they pick you up for?" she asked him.

"Possession, with intent to sell," he replied, continuing. "I tried to be careful and never thought I could get busted, but I was stupid and sold to the wrong person."

"I guess you sure were." Then trying to bluff him into admitting if he was a son of her boss, she asked, "Does your father know you're here?"

With that question, he turned as white as a ghost. Recovering his composure, he whisper to her. "Please keep your voice down. If the other prisoners find out who my dad is, I'll get beat the hell up, not to mention what my dad will do. He'll probably beat me even worse. Please don't tell him. Promise me," he begged. True fear was in his eyes.

Max thought about it for a couple of seconds, then told him. "Okay, I promise, I won't tell your dad your locked up here. But you know he's going to find out sooner or later."

As she turned to walk away, Sammy said, "Thank you. If and when I get out I promise I'll be better to Pam. Just don't tell my dad about me being in here, please. Remember, you promised me."

"Sure," she replied, "Like I said, I won't tell your dad you're here," she told him as she started walking back down the corridor to the booking sergeant. Arriving at his station, she proceeded to sign out. Handing him the clipboard back, she told him, "Your John Doe's name is Sammy O'Brien. Just thought I'd let you know." The desk sergeant looked up in recognition of the name, as she walked by his desk and headed to the elevator.

*I promised I wouldn't tell his father and I fully intend to keep my promise,* she thought to herself, smiling as she walked away. *I always keep my promises.*

Taking the elevator up to the fifth floor, she walked to her cubicle. She knew that she better check her messages and see if she had return call from Ross Lewis, the victim's son. She was gratified to see that he had returned her call and set up an appointment to meet with her on campus at his research laboratory. Once she had the time and location for her meeting, she checked to find the location on her phone in order to find the easiest route to get there.

With everything in place, she sat back and checked for any messages possibly from her daughter, that she might have. There were none. She then went through her notes on the case, to see if any new information popped out at her about her case. Nothing did.

With nothing else to do, she started walking around the other cubicles and introduced herself to the other officers who were there working. Most of the officers were pleasant and welcomed her, but when she told them she was Murphy's partner, she could tell by the change in their attitude, that they almost felt sorry for her. Most of them told her to stick with it, that things will get better. A few of them flat out told her, "I'm sorry to hear they teamed you up with Murphy."

There were several other female officers that she met and struck up an acquaintance with. They all welcomed her to the station and pumped her for information on her personal life. After awhile, Max noticed that the time had slipped away from her and that she needed to leave to meet with Ross Lewis at UCLA.

Driving to the UCLA campus, she found the building where she was scheduled to meet with Ross. 'Burton Medical and Cryogenics Research Institute' was the name on the front of the impressive building that Max was looking for. Finding a place to park, she entered into the building and went up to the receptionist desk. She identified herself and was given directions on where to find Ross Lewis. Following the directions, Max found herself in front of a completely glassed in laboratory, with several people, wearing lab coats and masks, working inside the sterile environment.

Tapping on the glass door until someone noticed her, she held up her police badge and mouth the words, 'Ross Lewis.' It took only a few moments before a twenty four year old, handsome young man, dressed in a white lab coat, came to the isolation door, swiped an ID badge and stepped through the isolation chamber door and then exited the room into the hallway to meet Max.

Shaking Max's hand, he introduced himself and asked how he could help her. Max was hesitant to ask if he knew about his father's death and the wounding of his stepmother. Fortunately, he brought up the subject first. "I guess you're here about my father's death." Max felt relieved that he already knew, but she was curious about who told him the bad news. She knew Murphy hadn't.

"Yes, I am," she replied, "But first I want to extend my sympathy about the loss of your father and the injury to your stepmother," she began with, "But there are a few things we need to clear up," she added.

Ross interrupted her. "First of all, you probably know or should know, that I didn't get along with Mary at all. My dad was infatuated with her even though she was only a year or two older than me. My dad was disappointed when he realized that neither I or my sister could tolerate her, so if your looking for motive to kill my stepmother, you need to look no farther then me. However, we loved our dad and had no motive to kill him. So, to save my time and yours, if you're looking for any one with a motive to kill them, rest assured, I have one for Mary but not on for my dad.

Max just stood there, amazed at Ross' admission of motive. For a moment she was at a loss for words. Recovering herself, she asked if he had an alibi for the afternoon of the crime.

Ross replied immediately. "Yes I do, I was right here in the lab with my colleagues. I can give you their names and contact information. I'm sure they will verify I was here all afternoon. Besides that, we have to swipe our ID cards to enter and exit the lab which is electronically logged in, so if you want, you can get a print out of my comings and goings from security."

Max was satisfied with Ross' alibi, but decided she would contact security and his colleagues to verify it, just to make sure. Continuing her questioning, she asked. "By the way, who called you to inform you of the murders? Was it your sister?"

Ross, without hesitation, replied. "No, not my sister. In case you didn't notice, Lisa is a basket case, and on a good day she might be able to tie her shoe laces. All Lisa can do is get through a day without an incident that ruins her perfect, idyllic, little world. The person who notified me was my dad's ex- mistress, Francine Jackson. In fact, Lisa is staying with her for a while, since our house is now a crime scene and off limits. So, is there anything else I can help you with?"

"No, that just about covers everything, it think." Handing him one of her cards. "If I can think of anything else, I'll contact you and if you could send me your co-workers names and phone numbers, my contact number and e-mail address is on the card." Pausing, " By the way, what do you do here in the lab?" she asked.

"Cryogenic research on transplant organs. We're trying to figure out a way to

use cryogenics to preserve organs, defrost them and keep them viable for extended periods of time. If we're successful it will save hundreds, maybe thousands of lives," he explained to her.

"Sound like a noble purpose. Good luck," Max told him.

"Thanks," Ross replied, as he headed back to the research lab.

Finishing up with Ross, she decided to find a place to eat before heading back to the precinct. Finding a fast food restaurant near by, she sat inside to eat her meal. While there, she decided to call her daughter at Berkeley. Finally reaching her on the phone, she enjoyed talking to Alexandria, updating her on her life and finding out what was going on in her world.

After the lunch, she headed back to the precinct. Arriving at her cubicle, she began going through the information she had obtained from Ross Lewis. After finishing transferring her notes to her computer, she checked for any phone messages. There were two. The first one was from the doctor at Mary Lewis' hospital. The doctor's message was that Mary Lewis was out of critical care and in a recovery room, and that she could have visitors on the following morning. Max thought that this was the first good break in the case. The second was an email from Ross Lewis with the names and telephone numbers of his co-workers needed to verify his alibi.

Max decided to call the co-workers first thing in the morning and get Ross Lewis' alibi out of the way. Then she would head over to the hospital and try get Mary Lewis' statement. She was hopeful at the least, that she would get valuable information about the attack on the family, and at best identify who assaulted her. Foe the rest of the afternoon she continued going through everything in her notes and trying to figure out what questions she would ask Mary Lewis in the following morning. She thought that if she checked with the forensic department on Mary Lewis' clothing the following afternoon, that it would give them plenty of time to analyze the results for her.

She knew that her vacation from Murphy would be over soon and that her captain's deadline for the case to be wrapped up in a few more days, was looming in the near future. She hoped that forensics would provide a clue, any clue, to breaking this case. At the end of the day, Max felt that her game plan for the next day, was in place.

Arriving at her apartment after work, she began fixing her supper, when there was a knock on her door. She knew that it had to be Pam from the next door apartment. Answering the door, she was met by her neighbor, who was in an agitated state. Pam was edgy, soaked in perpetration and had dilated pupils. Immediately, Max recognized the symptoms of drug withdrawal. "Did you find him? Is he coming home soon?" she questioned her aggressively. Max was taken aback by her appearance and abruptness. "Yes, I found him. He's being held in the Beverly Hills precinct on a possession and distribution charges. He should be arraigned within forty eight hours and can bail out. So you should have him back in a couple of days," she told Pam.

"A couple of days? No, you don't understand. I need him back. I can't wait a couple of days for him. I need him now," she said, almost screaming insistently .

A silence followed Pam's outburst between the two of them. Finally the tension between them broke. "How long have you been using?" Max asked her.

With that question, Pam broke completely down, crying and sobbing, while standing in Max's doorway. Taking her hand, she led Pam into her apartment and sat her down at the kitchen table.

"Okay, tell me everything," Max asked, handing a tissue to Pam to dry her eyes. It took a couple of minutes and several more tissues before Pam could talk coherently. " I met Sammy about two years ago at a night club. He was cute, smart, a good kisser, using coke and some how talked me into trying it. It wasn't long before I was hooked. I had no idea that Sammy was distributing on the street. If I tell you this, you got to promise you won't arrest me," Pam told her.

"Okay. I promise I won't," Max assured her.

"Sammy even had me moving drugs on the street for him. He had me delivering his drug sales because he thought nobody would suspect me. When I told him that a police officer lived next door to me, he though it would be the perfect cover for him to move in with me. No body would suspect a drug dealer living next door to a cop," she informed Max.

"I think he was just using you, because if you got caught with the drugs, you would never rat him out. He was just protecting himself, not you," Max explained to her. "You need to look out for yourself, not him. If you keep it up, you're going to be sitting in jail, along side of Sammy."

"I know that, but with Sammy in jail, I need to find a fix. I'm coming down and there's no more coke in the apartment. I need to find something soon, and besides that, I have no money" Pam told her. By now, she started shaking and sweating profusely.

"Well, I definitely don't have anything here that you can use, and I'm not going to give you money for a fix. What I will do is take you to a half way house where there a people who can help you. That is, if you want help." Max told her.

Pam sat at the table, shaking and sweating for several minutes as she thought about her options. Finally putting her hands to her face and crying, told Max. "Okay, whatever you think is right."

Max put her hand on her shoulder and told her, "Right choice. Let's go get you some help."

Getting her car keys, she walked Pam to Max's car and took her to the closest half way house that had a recovery program. Getting her signed in and settled, she headed back to her apartment, had supper and a good night sleep since there were nobody in the next door apartment to keep her awake.

The next morning, Max awoke rested and refreshed. Driving into work, she steeled herself to get through her agenda today, knowing that Murphy would soon be back the following day. Arriving at her cubicle, she checked for any messages. There were none. She then checked the names and contact numbers of Ross Lewis' co-workers to follow up on his alibi. Calling them, they all verified that Ross was at work with them during the time of his father's murder. Scratching him off the list, she headed to the hospital to interview the now conscience Mary Lewis.

Arriving at the hospital, she headed up to Mary's floor. At the nurse's station, she asked to see Mary's doctor. She was told that the doctor was in Mary Lewis' room, trying to save her life.

This puzzled Max as he thought Mary was supposed to be on the way to recovery. "What happened?" she asked the desk nurse. The nurse paused for several moments, hesitating as to whether or not she could give out any information. It wasn't until Max showed the nurse her badge, that the nurse beckoned Max to the side of the nurse's desk. Whispering to Max so that no could hear what she was saying, she told Max, " There was an attempt on her life last night. Somebody entered her room and injected air into her IV line. You might ask her doctor to let you see the video. That's all I can tell you, and I probably shouldn't have told you that much. I'm sure the doctor can tell you much more."

Max was taken aback and shocked, "What?" was all that came out of her mouth. The nurse just nodded in affirmation. Max asked her when the doctor would be available, and was informed that it could be awhile before the doctor could contact her. Max took out her business card and gave it to the nurse. " Can you have the doctor call me when he is available?"

"Will do." the nurse assured her.

# Chapter 7

Max left the hospital confused and mad. It was bad enough that a person or persons unknown had already killed three people and tried to kill Mary Lewis, not once, but twice, but what really infuriated her was the fact that it has happened the second time, almost right under her nose.

She called the precinct and arranged to have an officer stationed in front of Mary Lewis' hospital room for her protection. *Nothing like closing the barn door after the cows got out,* she thought to herself. She also realized that her schedule for the day was shot to hell.

*"Might as well see what forensics has for me,* she thought. Heading back to the 48th Precinct, she went up to the second floor. Entering the front reception area, she showed her badge and signed in at the desk. She was told that the person in charge of her case was Gemma Jefferies and was given directions to her lab.

Arriving at the lab, she was greeted by Jefferies, who escorted her onto her laboratory.

"Got any good news for me?" Max asked, her hopefully.

"Well," Jefferies began, "Yes and no. Unfortunately, the pool water and fish pond water destroyed any chance of evidence on three of the bodies, but thankfully, Mary Lewis' clothing proved a little more helpful. We found epithelial cells on the clothing and on the ground around her body, consistent with those of the daughter. However, this was to be expected as she was the one who discovered the body."

Max saw the logic of the epithelial cells and the lack of evidence caused by the water the victims were found in. She was starting to believe that some how, someone had possibly gotten away with the perfect murder. However she quickly swept that idea from her mind. Hopefully, she believed, forensics might still be helpful as she thought of more questions for Gemma.

"Did you find what caused the wounds?" she asked. "The autopsy seemed to indicate bullet holes but no bullets were found, nor any of the fired shell casings were located. I started thinking that maybe another type of weapon might have been used."

"What type of weapon are you thinking?" Gemma asked.

"I was thinking about something like a maybe a hunting crossbow. The wound hole is consistent with the shaft of a crossbow arrow. Couldn't the victims have been shot with a crossbow arrow and then the arrow removed by the assailant? Or perhaps some type of a dagger or knife with a round blade? Maybe something like a fishing spear gun?" Max asked, grasping at ideas.

Gemma paused for several moments. Max could tell by the look on her face, that her suggestions had raised some questions in her mind.

"Possibly a viable alternative. I'm will have to run a couple of tests to check out your theories, but there's one fly in the ointment." Gemma told her.

"What's that?" Max questioned.

"It's the gunpowder residue on the back of the blouse of Mary Lewis. A crossbow or knife wouldn't use gunpowder or leave any type of residue." Gemma explained.

The issue of the gunpowder residue set off an alarm in Max's mind. She knew there was something about it that was important, but it's importance escaped her for the moment.

Just then, Max's cell phone went off. Excusing herself she took the call. It was a nurse from the hospital telling her that Mary Lewis and her baby didn't survive the doctor's attempt to save her life.

"Baby? Mrs. Lewis was pregnant?" Max asked, astounded.

"If you have any questions, you'll have to talk to her doctor, and the doctor told me to tell you that you need to see the CCTV video that was recorded during the attack on Mrs. Lewis when you get here." the nurse informed her.

"I'll be at the hospital in an half an hour," she told the nurse. Terminating the call, she looked at Gemma. "I guess you heard the news. Seems my only witness is dead. Now I really need you to run your tests, and it appears now that she was pregnant. Can you run a DNA test on the fetus? I want to verify who the father is."

"Certainly. Have the hospital send over a DNA sample, and I'll give it top priority," Gemma told her.

Leaving the forensic department, she headed back to the hospital. Finding Mary Lewis' doctor took a couple of minutes. Finally he appeared, and ready to answer Max's questions. Guiding Max to his office, he closed the door, indicated for Max to take a chair as he seated himself behind the desk. "I'm sure you have a lot of questions, detective, so let me have them." the doctor told her.

"Sure do," Max replied, continuing, "First of all, tell me about the baby."

The doctor looked at his notes, then told her, "Mrs. Lewis was approximately four to six weeks pregnant. She probably didn't even know she was expecting. We only caught it from when her blood work came back from the lab."

"How did she react when you told her?" Max asked.

"Never had a chance to tell her," he told her.

"Could you please send DNA from the fetus over to the Beverly Hills Forensic

Department?" she requested.

"I anticipated your request and sent it over an hour ago," the doctor informed her.

Max thanked him and started to ask her next question. However, the doctor broke her

thought process, as he pulled a laptop computer and set it on his desk.

"You might want to look at the video that our CCTV cameras caught in the corridor

the night that Mrs. Lewis was attacked, detective," the doctor informed her. Max had

forgotten all about the video that the nurse had mentioned earlier. Sitting back in her

chair, she watched as the doctor opened his laptop computer, and turned it around on his desk so Max could see the screen. He then came out from behind his desk, and standing next to Max, turned it on. Finding the program that he wanted, pushed the play button. Max watched a video of the hospital hallway as nurses and doctors carried out their duties. She observed several nurses entering and exiting Mrs.

Lewis' room, through out the video until the point where an emergency alarm sounded and the doctor and three nurses ran into the room. After watching the entire video, Max was perplexed as to what she was suppose to see that was out of place on the video.

"Everything looked normal to me right up to the end," Max told him.

"At first I thought so too," the doctor explained. He then backed up the video and

started to play it forward again, only in slow motion.

"I know each and every doctor and nurse on this floor. I even know the aides and the

janitors who work on the floor, but I don't know this nurse," he told her as he hit the

freeze button on the computer.

Max was looking at a picture of a tall, long haired woman, wearing a surgical mask,

carrying a covered tray, coming out of Mrs. Lewis' room.

"What's so special about this nurse? Couldn't she be from another floor? Max asked.

"Maybe, but understand this; our nurses work hard and are on their feet all day, so they

wear sneakers and other types of comfortable shoes," he explained as he started

zooming in on the computer picture, "But not men's dress shoes."

Max looked at the feet of the nurse and observed she was wearing a pair of men's

black dress shoes.

"Doc, you should have been a detective. I never would have caught that," she told him.

"There were other clues besides the shoes. For one, the long flowing hair style is not

allowed on the hospital floor. The nurses have to tie the hair up or wear a hair net for

safety and health reasons. If you look closely you can tell it's a wig because the sideburns

are showing on the side of the face and lastly, the surgical mask would never be worn

except for a patient with a communicable disease, which Mrs. Lewis was not.

Max stood there for several moments, realizing that the photo might be that of the

person who killed her other victims, also.

"Doc, could I get a copy of this video for my forensic people to look at?" she

requested.

"Not a problem. I'll make you copy right now," he told her as he went to his desk

drawer, took out a small flash drive and put into the port on the side of the laptop. A few

seconds later he took the flash drive out and handed it to Max. Placing it in a small

evidence bag, she sealed it and initialed it, then put it safely in her pocket.

"Thanks Doc. You've been a great help. You know, you really would make a great

detective," she sincerely told him.

"Thanks, I do read a lot of detective novels. I guess they just rubbed off on me," the

doctor told her. Max just smiled.

Max left the hospital and headed back to deliver the flash drive to Gemma and see if

she had any good news for her. Signing in, she went straight to her office. Upon arriving she observed Gemma running some type of testing. Tapping on the window of the lab, Max finally caught her attention. Looking up from her project she was working on, she saw Max and beckoned her to come in.

Walking in to the lab, Max asked. "Did you get the DNA sample from the hospital?"

"About forty five minutes ago. We started the processing but you should know that it takes about twelve hours to get results. So we won't have any news for you until tomorrow morning." Gemma informed her.

"Great, but I also have a couple of other things I need done." Max told her, handing her the flash drive the doctor at the hospital gave her.

"What are we looking for?" Gemma asked.

"Anything that might help identify the nurse wearing the surgical mask and the men's dress shoes." Max explained.

"That's interesting," Gemma stated as she examined the envelope with the flash drive in it.

"Oh, and one other thing. Could you call the coroner's office and get a DNA sample from Mr. Lewis and compare it to the baby's DNA?" Max inquired.

"Paternity test?" Gemma asked,

"Just a gut feeling," Max responded.

"With the other cases we have, you know we are going to have to work all night for you, don't you?" Gemma told Max.

"What do you mean by we?" Max questioned.

"My assistant, Phil over there," pointing to her assistant who was busily at work. "Phil is on an hourly basis, and will love the overtime. However, I am salary and won't," she explained to Max. "And just to let you know, I'm not worth a damn until I get my coffee in the morning."

"Consider that noted. I'll take care of the coffee tomorrow morning." Max told her, as she headed out the door.

Max left Forensic and rode the elevator up to the top floor. Walking over to her cubicle, she observed a large paper banner on the wall over her desk. 'Vacation is over tomorrow, Rookie,' with a smiley face drawn on it. At first Max was annoyed about it until Frank and several other detectives popped into her area with a dozen cupcakes.

"We thought you might need a sugar boost to get ready for tomorrow." Frank good naturally explained to her, giving her a pat on the back. The other detectives followed suite, each one giving her words of encouragement. Max thanked each one of them respectively.

Finally after everyone had left except Frank, Max sat in her chair and took a deep breath. "Thanks Frank, I really needed that. But what I don't need is this," she told him as she proceeded to tear the banner down.

"I didn't do anything special," Frank stated, helping her fold up the paper banner He then threw the banner into the trash can.

"It was special to me," Max told him with a smile.

"Well, just about everyone here is rooting for you. Not to change the subject, but how are you going to deal with Murphy tomorrow?" Frank inquired.

"Don't know. Just take it one day at a time. If I'm lucky, maybe he'll put his foot in his mouth again and get another vacation." Max told him.

"We could only be so lucky," he added. "Not to change the subject again, but how is your investigation going? The boss keeps asking about it."

Max told him all of the details of her case, not leaving out anything. She knew that Frank was the one person who had Captain's O'Brien's ear and by telling him everything, knew that it would all go right back to the captain. This didn't bother her, too much.

Frank took a couple of moments, digesting everything that Max had told him. Finally speaking, he told her. "Finish your paperwork and let me know when you're done, then I'll take you to dinner."

"Sounds good, but this time I buy" Max replied to him, with a smile.

Dinner with Frank was a relaxing time. He had picked a small diner a couple of blocks from the precinct. When they walked into it the waitress knew Frank by name when she came to wait on them in their booth.

Frank was extremely talkative, telling Max about his new live-in partner who was a stock broker in one of the brokerage houses in downtown Los Angeles. Frank revealed to her, that he came from a small town in northern California and spent all about his life growing up there. He even shared the reasons about why he became a detective.

Max told him about being born and raised in a small Midwestern town, joining the military and all about her two husbands. She even told him the reasons why she didn't drink, leaving some of the seedy details out that she didn't feel he needed to know.

By the time they had finished dinner and started walking back to the precinct to get their cars, Max told him that she appreciated him taking her under his wing and she really welcomed having him as a good friend. As they were about to part to go to their cars, Max asked. "I know you report back to O'Brien, so how much of this evening is going back to him?"

Frank gave her a huge grin and stated. "What happens on the job goes to O'Brien, but what happens with my friends, stays with me. Good night, friend."

"Thanks, friend," Max responded with a smile.

# Chapter 8

Max had restless night. She tossed and turned through out the night until sometime in the early morning she finally fell asleep. Waking when her alarm went off, she jumped out of bed, showered and dressed and hurriedly headed to work. Stopping at a near by coffee shop on the way in, she remembered to pick up coffee for herself and the Forensics crew.

Arriving at work, she headed to her cubicle, carefully balancing the three hot coffees in the cardboard cup holder the coffee shop had provided. She saw the back of someone sitting in her chair. *Please be Frank. Please, please be Frank.* Max thought to herself. Unfortunately, it wasn't.

Recognizing who it was, she put a fake smile on her face and walked into her cubicle.

"Morning Murphy, how was your vacation?" she asked, carefully placing the three coffee's on her desk. She observed that he had taken her notebook out of her desk and was leafing through it. At first she felt violated but then remembered that she had done the exact same to him. Putting her ego aside, she asked him. "Catching up on our case?" Murphy nodded his head affirmatively, as he flipped through another page of her notes, then threw the notebook onto her desk. "Looks like you've been busy while I've been gone, rookie." he said sarcastically, taking one of the coffee cups, removing the lid and taking a drink. Not realizing just how hot the coffee was, he burned the inside of his mouth and spitted some of it up onto her desk. *Serves him right,* she thought. *Didn't even bother to ask.*

"Watch out, it might be hot," Max told him. "The other two are for Forensics. I owe it to them for working all night on our case. She didn't bother telling him that the coffee he took was hers.

"Well, I guess they won't need this one," he said as he took the cup over to his desk, taking the lid off and blowing on it to try and cool it down.

*Looks like it's the same old Murphy.* She thought to herself, as she picked up her notebook, put it in her pocket, then picked up the two remaining coffee cups and started heading towards the forensic department.

"Where to, rookie?" Murphy asked.

"Forensics, you might want to come along so you can get caught up," she informed him.

"Sure, why not. Haven't got anything better to do," he replied.

They were both silent as they rode the elevator down to Forensics. Arriving at the Forensics floor, they exited the elevator and signed in at the reception desk. Max led the way to Gemma's lab. Walking in, she saw Gemma and Phil busily working on their projects. Setting the coffee on a counter, she loudly cleared her throat as Gemma and Phil had not noticed her and Murphy walking in.

They both looked up from the projects they were busy with. Gemma walked over to Max. Noticing the two coffee's on the counter, picked up one and called Phil over to get his cup. Taking a sip, Gemma asked Max, "Not a coffee drinker?" Max just gave Murphy a dirty look, which Murphy just ignored, and then she told her. "I'll get some later. Right now I just need to know if you got any results?"

"Well, yes and no. As far as your ideas on the cause of the wounds, nothing panned out. We still have no idea as to what caused them. However, your video shows your nurse is definitely a man. We were unable to determine age or facial recognition, but he is Caucasian and about six feet tall." Gemma revealed to her.

Max was disappointed at the results of the wounds, but felt better about the analysis of the video. "What about the DNA results?" she asked.

Gemma told her that Phil was working on that project. The three of them walked over to Phil's work station. "Phil, show them the result of the tests." Phil turned on a light screen mounted on the wall. Taking a transparency about the size of a sheet of paper and sliding it on to the screen, he explained. "This is the DNA of Mr. Lewis."

To Max, the transparency looked like several rows of different multicolored boxes. Phil then slide a second transparency next to the first one so they were side by side. Comparing them, to her they looked almost identical. Phil then explained what they were looking at.

"Comparing the two slides, I can confirm that the DNA from the fetus is related to the DNA of Mr. Lewis."

With this revelation, Murphy became agitated to the point of almost shouting "What a waste of time. I knew this crap wouldn't pan out. Come on, Rookie, we're going to solve this case the old fashioned way with plain, good old fashion detective work," he told Max as he pushed her by the shoulder out the door and back to the elevator.

Max was so shocked by Murphy's abrupt departure from Forensics,and the way he man-handled her, that she was speechless. By the time they got off the elevator, she was fuming. Finally finding her voice, she began tearing into Murphy. "You are the most stupidest, bull headed, ill mannered person I have ever met. You are gone for three days while I'm working my ass off, trying to solve our case, and you go and dismiss the evidence I gathered. You have to be the most obnoxious person I have ever worked with."

Murphy just kept on walking, ignoring her tirade, leaving Max standing frustrated by the elevator doors. Neither she or Murphy noticed Captain O'Brien standing with the group of people watching Max's meltdown. Nor did she see the frown upon his face as he turned to go back to his office.

Finally Frank stepped out of the group of observers, walked over to Max, and told her to go to the bathroom and cool down. Realizing that he was right, she thanked him and went into the ladies bathroom. Taking a wet paper towel, she wiped down her face, which helped her to calm down. Walking back onto the floor, she quickly moved to her cubicle, preparing mentally to have round two with Murphy. Fortunately, Murphy was nowhere to be seen. Frank and the other detectives were leaving her some space so she could catch her breath and relax.

Her respite of solitude only lasted for about fifteen minutes. Frank popped into her cubicle and asked. "You Okay?"

"Yeah, I guess I just let Murphy get to me. I tell you, it's almost like he goes out of his way to antagonize me, and I don't know why."

"I'll tell you why and it's not what you think. Murphy is a lone wolf, and always has been. The only way he keeps his job is by solving cases on his own. That way, he gets all the glory and recognition. If he has a partner that might be more intelligent and smarter than him, it detracts from his spotlight. So his policy is to run off any partner that might possibly steal his thunder. You, Maxine Somers, steal his thunder, and by the way, our boss wants to see you now." Frank informed her.

"Does he hear about my meltdown?" Max asked.

"Heard and saw it," Frank told her.

"Is he upset?" Max wanted to know.

"He's hard to read sometimes. I can't tell if he's upset with you or Murphy," Frank explained. "Whatever the case, I'd get over to his office now and face the music."

"I guess you're right," she said. "Just wish I knew if it's a waltz or a funeral march."

Frank laughed at Max's attempt at humor. "You won't know until you hear the music."

"Guess you're right. Wish me luck." Max requested of him.

"Good luck," Frank wished her, as Max headed over to O'Brien's office.

Arriving at the captain's office, she took a deep breath before knocking on the door.

"Get in here, Somers. Is Murphy with you?" O'Brien barked, before she had the chance.

"No sir, just Somers," she informed him, as she opened the door and walked in.

Before she could even sit down, O'Brien started on her. "Explain to me exactly what the hell was going on at the elevator between you and Murphy, and you better make it good."

Max then informed him the details leading up to her losing her temper at Murphy, leaving none of the details out, starting with him not following through on verifying alibis, all the way to the coffee incident and then his dismissing the forensics evidence that could break the case.

O'Brien appeared to listen to her story, but Max got the distinct feeling that his mind really wasn't listening to her but was focused a million miles away, thinking of something else. Max finished documenting her complaints, which seemed to snap O'Brien back to the issue at hand. Picking up and shuffling some papers, he finally cleared his throat and gruffly lectured her. "Listen Detective Somers, I got too many problems running this precinct without two of my people slugging it out, especially in front of the rest of the squad. If you want another partner, I have to tell you, I just can't swing that right now. I would have to bench you on a desk or put you undercover, a least until I have a senior detective lose a partner. That would open up a position for you to work with, or you and Murphy are going to have to play nice until something opens up," he explained, continuing,

"Look, I know Murphy is a handful and he has a track record to prove it. So, I do understand your frustration and anger. Believe me, you're not the first person to have trouble with him. But if you can just tough it out, I can promise you that he will be retiring soon. If you can't, just promise me you'll shoot him someplace away from the precinct."

After saying the last part, he actually gave Max a smile.

"Thank you, Sir. I appreciate you patience and your advice. I want you to know that I think I can work with Murphy, but he makes it damn hard to do so. I can't promise that my anger won't get the best of me again, but I can promise you, I won't shoot him, at least not in this building." Max replied.

"Good, that's settled. Now get out of here and send Murphy to me when you see him. I sent Forester to find him twenty minutes ago but obviously Forester hasn't made it to Mike's Bar down the street to locate him." O'Neil informed her.

'Yes Sir, if I see him, I give him your message. I'll even head over to Mike's and see if he's there," she told him as she left his office.

Heading to the elevator, she spotted Frank coming from the break room. "I take it you haven't found Murphy?" she asked.

"So far, no. I was just heading to his favorite bar and see if he's taking an early lunch break. How did your lecture from O'Brien go?" Frank inquired.

"I'm still here," she told him, confidently.

"Good. Most don't come back from one of O'Brien's lectures," he informed her.

" I can believe that. Look, I'll go over to Mike's for you, and see if he's there." she informed him.

"Should I send the EMS people over there in about fifteen minutes," Frank joked.

"Not necessary, but if you don't see me in an hour, send help for me," she quipped.

Walking down the street fifteen minutes later, the experience of entering into Mike's Bar felt like a familiar experience from her old drinking days. The smell was always the same, stale cigarette smoke and stale beer. The dimly lit bar was almost empty because of the early hour. Even so, several patrons were at the bar drinking or sitting at a table, playing cards. Max spotted Murphy at the end of the bar, sitting by himself, a half empty beer glass in front of him.

Slowly walking up to him, she pulled up the stool next to him and sat down. The bartender approached her for her order, but she waved him away. He left the two of them alone.

Without looking at her, Murphy started the conversation. "O'Brien chew you out?"

"Yup" Max replied

"And you're still here?" he questioned.

"Yup," she said.

"Impressive. Guess it"s my turn?" he asked.

"Yup," she informed him.

"Suppose I better get back and take my licks," Murphy told her as he started finishing his beer.

"Take you time. O'Brien isn't going any where for awhile," she told him as she slid a box of breath fresheners down the bar to him.

Taking several of them out of the box, he finished the rest of his beer and then popped the breath fresheners into his mouth. The bartender came down to refresh his drink, but Murphy just told him, "That's it for me, Bobby. Put it on my tab."

The bartender nodded, picked up the empty glass and took it to the sink to clean.

"How bad?" Murphy asked her.

"Not bad. I've had worse when I was in the military," she told him.

"You were in the military? Murphy questioned, as his adversarial tone changed. "Which branch?

Max unbutton her sleeve and rolled it up, showing him her army tattoo. "Afghanistan- two tours," she proudly told him. "Kandahar."

"And I thought you were some college pansy, playing detective to sooth your social conscience," he told her, "Guess I got you wrong," he told her as he rolled up his sleeve to show her his marine tattoo."

"See any action?" Max inquired.

"More than I wanted, but I really don't want to talk about it," he quietly told her.

"Nam?" was all Max asked.

Murphy didn't reply but just nodded his head. Max noticed that his eyes started to slightly well up with tears. He then grabbed a bar towel and wiped his eyes. "Allergies," was all he said. "Guess we better get back. By the way- thanks for the mouth fresheners, but it won't make any difference, O'Brien knows where I am, right?"

"I'm afraid you're right about that. You better find a different place to have your lunch break if you don't want to be found," Max suggested to him.

"Nah, this is the only bar to let me put my lunch on a tab," he explained to Max with a smile.

She had to laugh at his response. The two of them walked back to the precinct together, actually having a cordial conversation. Max thought that maybe things might be different now between the two of them. She was wrong. As soon as they entered into the police precinct, it was like a switch was thrown and the old Murphy was back. This was when she realized that Murphy's rough nature was only an illusion, a persona. She thought she could finally work with Murphy, knowing that as long as he didn't cross over any lines, she would be fine.

Getting off the elevator on the top floor, Murphy told Max, "I'll be with the Captain if you need me, rookie," loud enough for just about everybody to hear him. As he headed towards O'Brien's office. Max just shook her head.

Heading towards her cubicle, she ran into Frank who was talking with another detective. Finishing up his conversation, he asked Max. "I take it you found him?"

"Yeah, he was taking an early liquid lunch break," Max assured him.

Frank looked her over and then said, "I don't see any blood. He must still be alive."

"For now," Max told him. "But no promises he's going to stay that way."

"What now?" Frank asked, smiling because of Max's comment.

"I guess after he gets done with the captain, we'll have to sit down together and try to figure out the next step in the investigation." Max explained. "That won't take long because we really don't have much to go on," she added.

"Forensics wasn't much help?" Frank questioned.

"No, not much. We still don't know what kind of weapon was used or why there were no bullets found in our victims. We don't even know why they were killed. All we do know is that whoever did it, wanted them all dead so bad, that they made a second try on Mrs. Lewis and succeeded. And your not going to believe me when I tell you that the second attempt was made by an unknown nurse wearing a wig and men's shoes," she told Frank dejectedly.

Frank thought for a minute, then told Max. "When you got nothing to go on, then go back to the beginning. Did you completely search the house and grounds for a weapon? If not, maybe it's still there. Re-interview everybody, hopefully maybe they'll remember something new, and most of all, keep following the money."

Max thought about what Frank said and realized that he was right. Thanking him for his advice, she headed to her cubicle and started re-reading her notes again. After reading them, she thought to herself, *What am I missing? Something doesn't feel right about the case because there wasn't any logical reason for everybody to be killed. Maybe Mr. Lewis, or maybe Mary Lewis. But why kill the gardener and the maid?*

Then it hit her, *Because everybody knew who the killer was. They would have known and recognized the murderer if they survived*, she thought to herself. *Frank was right, we have to go back to the beginning.*

Just as she had the revelation, Murphy showed up to his desk. Seeing him back, she went to his cubicle and informed him, "We have to back to the Lewis house, we need a more complete search of the house and grounds and we also need to re-interview everybody involved."

"Why?" Murphy questioned.

"Because we have nothing as far as evidence except for the fact that all of our victims must have known the killer," Max explained to him. "We're not only missing something besides a weapon and bullets, we're missing a motive. I'm pretty sure that this case has nothing to do with drugs or money. So, what else is there? What's left?" She questioned.

Murphy sat for a moment thinking, and quietly said, "Revenge."

# Chapter 9

Max and Murphy, in a rare moment of cooperation, spent the rest of the afternoon planning an agenda and formulating the questions they had to have answers to. Finishing up, Max told Murphy she was heading home and she would meet him at the office first thing in the morning. Murphy told her he was going to Mike's Bar for some late lunch.

"Don't have too much lunch. You need to be sharp tomorrow. And stay away from the bad buffalo wings," she advised him with a smile.

Murphy seemed to take her advice well, telling her, "Remember what you told me about not controlling you?"

"Yeah, why?" Max responded.

"Well, don't tell me how much lunch I can have," he told her with a grin.

"That's fair," she responded, "See you in the morning, Murphy," as she headed toward the elevator.

Max arrived at her apartment and found a message on her answering machine from Pam. Calling her back at the halfway house, it took a few minutes for who ever answered to get Pam to the phone. "Detective Somers, is that you?" she asked.

"Yes Pam, what can I do for you?" Max asked.

"I tried to call Sammy at your precinct yesterday and was informed that they had no prisoner there by that name. The person on the precinct phone told me that they never did have a prisoner by that name. When I questioned the guy, he got angry with me and hung up. I thought you told me that you talked to him when he was in holding?" she asked.

"I did. Are you sure you called the Beverly Hills Precinct?" Max asked.

"I asked them the same thing. They said it was Precinct 48, the Beverly Hills division." she explained to Max.

" Well that sounds like the right location. They told you he wasn't there? That's strange. Listen, I'm going to be busy most of tomorrow, but I'll try to sort it out as to where he is as soon as I can. By the way, how is your recovery working out for you?" Max inquired.

Pam paused for a moment, then told Max that everything was going good. She explained that the first day was kind of hard but the support and counseling seemed to help a lot.

"That's really good news, but listen, I'll have to get back to you late tomorrow, when and if, I find out anything about Sammy. Okay?" Max told her.

"Okay and thank you, Detective. When you talk to him, tell him I miss him and love him very much," she requested.

" I sure will," Max replied.

Hanging up the phone, Max tried to think what might have possibly happened to Sammy O'Brien since she saw him, and then promised to herself to get to the bottom of it when she finally had time, hopefully some time tomorrow.

Getting a good night sleep escaped Max, as she tossed and turned, watching the alarm clock slowly progress through the night. At some time early in the morning, she must have drifted off because she was dead to the world when her alarm finally went off.

Feeling groggy and cranky, she quickly jumped in the shower and forced down some breakfast. Driving into work, she went over in her mind what she and Murphy had scheduled for the day. Arriving at the precinct on time, she waited for Murphy to make an appearance. After waiting almost a hour and a half, he finally showed up, unshaven and disheveled. Max just rolled her eyes and realized he wasn't going to be of much help in the investigation.

"Ready to get on the street, partner?" she asked.

"Coffee, need coffee," Murphy grunted, as he headed toward the break room.

Her attitude didn't improve as she had to wait for Murphy to slowly sauntered into the break room and unhurriedly indulge himself in two cups of coffee. When he had finally finished, Max told him it was time to get on the road.

"Why? Where are we going?" he inquired. Max just took a deep breath and explained to him they had an agenda planned for the day.

"Oh yeah." he replied, as the conversation from the previous day came back to him..

Max interrupted his thoughts," O'Brien has us on a deadline to clear this case, so we really are up against the wall to solve it. We really have no time to waste, and by the way, how come you were so late this morning?" she asked.

"Late lunch." was all he said.

Max held her breath in frustration, but held her temper in check. She thought of several comments she would like to make, but decided it would really be best not to say anything so as not to start an argument.

"We need to get back to our crime scene and do a more comprehensive search of the house and grounds. I'm pretty sure we overlooked something." Max explained as they drove out of the precinct parking garage.

"Okay, sounds like a plan. Wake me up when we get there." Murphy requested as he put his head against the side window and fell asleep.

Arriving back at the crime scene, she woke Murphy up from his slumber. As they got out of the car, Max took it upon herself to refresh the assigned search details to Murphy. "I think we need to re-search the pool and grounds to see if there is possibly anything we missed. After we're done, we can go through the house," she suggested. Murphy only grunted in response but followed her directions,

Walking up to the house, Max brushed the yellow crime scene tape away and opened the lock box on the door handle. Retrieving the house key, she opened the front door and walked in. The house had a slightly musty smell as it had no air conditioning running for the few days its been empty since the murders.

Reaching the pool doors, Max slide them open and she and Murphy spent the next hour searching the pool, deck, and lawn for anything that might be a helpful clue. They found nothing.

Going back into the house, Max divided the search into Murphy taking the ground level of the house and Max taking the bedrooms upstairs.

Murphy went into the kitchen and started his search while Max went up the stairs and started with the master bedroom. Finding nothing, she moved on to what appeared to be Ross' room. It looked perfectly normal but unused for some time.

There was a fine layer of dust on the furniture indicating to Max that no one had been in it for awhile, Tearing the room apart, she found nothing to help the case. Moving onto Lisa's bedroom, it looked exactly the same as when she interviewed her except the bed was made. Proceeding to search the room, Max remembered back to when she was a teenager, and where she hid her personal stuff from her parents. She began by tearing the desk apart, taking out the drawers and looking inside the drawer cavity and the bottom and back of each drawer, making sure noting was concealed in them. The next place she searched was the bed. Stripping the bed of its sheets and flipping the mattress over, she found what she was looking for. A small slit had been made in the bottom of the mattress and a small diary sized book was concealed within it. *Some things never change,* she thought to herself with a smile. She remembered doing the same thing as a teenager.

Pulling the diary out, she started to flip through it. It looked just like any teenage girl's diary until she got to about the middle of it. Max noticed that several pages had been ripped out. Flipping back through the pages and looking more closely, she found several other paged that had been removed. *That's strange,* she thought to herself. Noticing that there were indentations on the empty page next to where the last page had been removed, she took her pencil, and lightly rubbing over the indentations with the side of the pencil lead, manage to read what was written on the missing page. The words, 'I hate him' was written multiple times so that it appeared to fill the entire page.

*Somebody certainly has a lot of rage toward a man. I know who probably wrote this, but now to find out who the 'him' was. Time to re-interview the daughter,* Max thought to herself.

Max finished searching to second level of the mansion, finding nothing else of value, Going downstairs, she found Murphy searching through the den, leisurely.

"Find anything?" she asked him.

"Nah, just some spoiled yogurt in the refrigerator. Everything else is clean. How about you?" he replied.

"Found the daughter's diary. She has a lot of anger issues toward someone," Max said, showing him the restored page of the diary.

Murphy took the diary from Max and read what she had restored. "I guess we better talk with the daughter again. Do you know where we can find her?

"Her brother told me she was staying with Francine Jackson. You remember her? The CEO of Lewis Industries, the one that got you a three day vacation?" Max asked him, reveling on the pained look on Murphy's face.

"I think we better give Ms. Jackson a call and ask if she could bring Lisa in for a talk." Murphy suggested.

I'm thinking you're right, but since she's a minor, she might want to bring a lawyer with her too." Max advised.

"Good idea, and since Jackson gets along so well with you, I think you should make the call," Murphy suggested.

"Not a problem," she told him, continuing, " Best to keep you and her separated as much as possible. I don't think you want another vacation from O'Brien, do you? Look, I have business to do back at the precinct after I make the call. I'll set the meeting up for as soon as I can so don't be heading out for your regular lunch today. I need you on your best behavior. I'm sure you don't want another three day vacation, do you?"

"Maybe," was all he replied, leaving Max wondering what shape he would be in for the interview.

Heading back to the precinct, Murphy was silent as was Max. Arriving back and riding the elevator, Max again reminded Murphy to be on his best behavior during the interview. Murphy just nodded his head.

Once in the office, they both headed to their cubicles. Max found the phone number for Francine Jackson and called her to ask if she could bring Lisa in to the precinct to answer a couple of questions. Jackson questioned her as to what it concerned. Max tried to be very vague, telling her that it was just to clear up a few loose ends, and then suggested that it might be a good idea to bring along a lawyer, if they wanted to. Jackson told Max that they would be there around three o'clock. Hanging up the phone, Max sensed she heard a touch of nervousness in Jackson's voice.

After getting off the phone, she turned and noticed that Murphy was standing behind her and was listening to her conversation. "You heard?" she asked him.

"Yeah, three o'clock. I guess that gives me a couple of hours to kill," he replied.

"Don't go to lunch at Mike's Bar," she warned him with a grin. Fortunately Murphy took it in a good good-natured way.

Max looked at her watch and noticed it was time for her lunch. She invited Murphy to join her in the break room but he declined with a smile. Max started to think that maybe working with Murphy wasn't going to be so bad after all.

Walking in to the break room, she saw Frank eating alone. She grabbed her lunch from the refrigerator and joined him at his table.

"How's it going?" he asked as Max sat down at the table.

"Not too bad. Might have a break in the murder case, and miracle of miracles, Murphy is actually cooperating with me on the case." Max told him.

Frank was silent for a couple of moments with a frown on his face. Max noticed it right away and asked. "What's wrong?"

"The last partner that Murphy worked with started out rough, but after a couple of weeks of frustration, Murphy started smiling and cooperating. His partner was gone a week later," he explained to Max. That statement didn't make Max feel secure. "Why? What happened?" Max asked.

"Don't know. All I know was that for no apparent reason, he turned in his resignation after three weeks of Murphy. He was reassigned to writing parking tickets downtown," Frank explained.

Max sat in stunned silence, evaluating what she had just been told.

"Three weeks?" Max finally commented.

"Three weeks," Frank stated with an air of finality.

Max sat in silence, eating her lunch, and contemplated Frank's words.

After a few minutes Frank saw the frown on Max's face and interrupted her thoughts.

"Don't worry. You're much tougher than the last one and a lot smarter. You're doing just fine. Don't let Murphy get to you," Frank reassured her.

"Thanks, that makes me feel so much better," Max told him sarcastically.

"Knew it would," Frank told her with a smile. Finishing up his lunch, he patted Max on the back and tried to put her at ease. "See you later," he told her as he left the break room.

Max finished her lunch and then took the elevator to the fourth floor where the booking and holding cells were. Going to the booking sergeant's desk, she noticed that instead of the original booking officer that Max had dealt with before, there was a female officer standing duty.

Introducing herself, she was told by the officer, "I know who you are, You're the new detective from the fifth floor, aren't you," she told Max.

"Yes, and I need your help finding a person being held in booking, probably waiting for arraignment," Max explained.

"Sure, you got a name for me?" the officer asked.

"He came in as a John Doe, but his real name is Sammy O'Brien. I think he was being help on possession with intent to distribute," Max explained to her.

The booking officer pulled out a clipboard that had names of the people being held in the cells. "No, no one by that name is showing," she told Max.

"Perhaps he was transferred to arraignment?" Max questioned.

Looking at more paperwork, she turned the paper work around so that Max could read it, the officer told her nobody by that name had been transported out to the court house within the last week.

This perplexed Max and told the booking officer, "That's strange, I just talked to him here in his cell here, a few days ago."

"All I have to go on is my paper work, and he's not showing up on it," the officer tersely explained to her. Max had to agree, seeing nothing in the paperwork to indicate Sammy had ever been there. Starting to leave, she had a second thought.

"Wait, do you have the log in sheet from three days ago?" she asked the officer.

"Sure do," she replied as she brought out a ledger file and opened it for Max to see. Max noticed that it appeared different than the form she had signed into a couple of days ago. Looking at the signatures and the dates, she noticed that it only contained information for the last two days. "Where are the pages from the last three or four days?" she asked.

"I think the old form was full, so they replaced it with a new one." the officer commented.

"Okay, then were is the old one?" Max inquired.

The booking officer looked around and in the desk, but finally admitted that it was no were to be found. "I don't seem to have it here. I know they never throw them away when they are full- you know, evidence and everything, but I have no idea where they go," she explained to Max. "You'll have to check with my sergeant."

Max thought it suspicious that someone replaced the old booking record, when she knew it was only about half full when she had just signed it a couple of days before.

"Where could it be if it's not here?" she asked.

"I don't know, perhaps the Chief has it." she told Max.

"Maybe- guess I could check with him," she replied, but she wasn't really sure if she wanted to go down that road right now, seeing she needed to solve the murder cases before confronting him.

"Thanks for your information, I'll check with him later," she said to the booking officer.

Heading back upstairs, she killed some time at her desk, waiting for Lisa Lewis to arrive.

Almost exactly three o'clock, the front reception desk called Max to inform her that she had visitors. Max informed Murphy, who actually came back from lunch early, that it was time to talk with Lisa Lewis, Francine Jackson and probably a lawyer.

Murphy suggested that it might be best if Max went and escorted them to the interrogation room since he had history with Jackson. Max for once, agreed with him.

Taking the elevator down to the ground floor, she saw Lisa and Ms, Jackson waiting at the reception desk. She put on her most pleasant smile and welcomed and thanked them for coming. "No lawyer?" Max asked casually, as they rode the elevator up to the top floor.

"Since Lisa is a minor with no appropriate relatives to take custody of her, I have petitioned the court to act as her guardian and attorney ad litem, at least until she reaches the age of majority." Jackson informed her.

" So you're acting as both her guardian and lawyer?" Max asked.

"For right now unofficially until the final papers are signed, which will be happening tomorrow. Then I'll be officially acting as such. Right not I'm just here as a friend and advisor," she replied.

Arriving at the top floor, Max guided Lisa and Jackson to the interrogating room. The interrogation room was a pleasant open room, with large windows which gave a spectacular view of the surrounding Los Angeles skyline. A large executive style table was surrounded by comfortable office chairs. The room was set up to handle twenty people or more easily so that multiple lawyers and police could hold conferences. There was a camera and microphones set up on the table for depositions and interrogation, and a large flat screen television mounted on one of the walls.

Getting Jackson and Lisa settled, Max turned on the camera on the table and aimed it so that both of them were in the frame.

"Why are you recording us? I thought this was just a friendly talk?" Ms. Jackson queried.

"It is," Max told her. " It's just that we need to clear up a couple of issues, and my boss wants an official recording of the interview," she explained.

"Fine, let's just cut to the chase and get this over with," Ms. Jackson told her, some what curtly.

"Good. First of all Lisa, I know that finding your parents and the others the way that you did, must have been a real shock for you. So I was just wondering if since then, you might have recalled any thing more as far as what you saw or heard," Max asked.

"No, nothing that I can recall," Lisa explained. Max noticed she squirmed a bit in the chair when she gave her answer.

"Okay, thank you. I only have one other question for you." Max told her as she slid Lisa's diary out of a manila folder. The look of panic swept across Lisa's face for a moment, then she quickly regained her composure. "Why do you have my diary?" she asked.

"I thought you might explain a certain page we recovered," Max questioned.

Taking a photo copy of the recovered page from the folder, Max slid it across the table so it stopped in front of Lisa. Looking down, Lisa's face turned red. Ms. Jackson immediately saw the reaction of Lisa and requested the interview be paused.

"Certainly," Max replied. " The interview is paused at three twenty at the request of the witness," she spoke for the microphone, then reached over and turned off the camera.

"Would you like the room?" she asked.

"Please, I think we need a ten minute break," Jackson requested. Max obliged them and left the room. Once outside, she was met by Murphy who had been watching and listening through a one way mirror and through a speaker. He had turned off the speaker as Max left the interrogation room.

" You sure got a reaction out of her with the diary," Murphy told her.

"Sure did. More than I expected." Max replied.

After a little over ten minutes later, Max knocked on the door and re-entered the interrogation room and asked, "Ready to resume?" Jackson and Lisa both nodded affirmatively. "Good," Max replied. Sitting down at the conference table, Max turned the camera back on. Speaking into the microphone, she resumed the interview. With all the formalities were done, Max asked, "So Lisa, can you explain and tell me who you are aiming your animosity at."

Ms. Jackson proceeded to speak as Lisa sat back in her chair. " Lisa was upset when her brother moved out of the house and left her alone to deal with her mother-in law alone. She was just venting her frustration toward him in her diary."

"Is that right, Lisa? You were just upset at your brother?" Max inquired.

Lisa looked at Ms. Jackson who nodded to her. She then leaned forward in her chair and spoke directly into the microphone. "Yes it is," she replied. "I was terribly upset to be stuck alone in that house with that horrible woman," she recited.

To Max, it sounded almost like she had memorized her statement. Pausing for a moment, she then announced, "Okay, that's it for me. I want to thank you for coming in for this interview and clearing this up. If you remember any thing else, please give me a call." Then speaking into the microphone, "This ends the interview of Lisa Lewis at three forty five." Rising from the table, she asked if they had any other questions, and offered to lead them to the elevator.

After Lisa and Ms. Jackson were in the elevator on the way down to the main floor, Murphy joined Max, as she was standing next to the elevator doors.

Well, were you watching? What did you think?" Max asked him.

"She lying like hell," Murphy replied. "All the tells were there. Shifting in her chair, the eye movement, even the tone of her voice are all evidence she's hiding something," he added.

"I agree. We need to talk to the brother again. Do you want to do it tomorrow?" she asked.

"You're on your own tomorrow morning. I'm scheduled to be in court for a case from a drug bust from about a year ago. I have to testify and can't get out of it. Can you handle it?" Murphy informed her.

"Sure, no problem." she reassured him.

# Chapter 10

The next morning Max arose early. She had made an appointment to interview Ross Lewis on the previous afternoon, and wanted to get an early start to the day. Arriving at work, she needed to talk to Gemma in Forensics before Murphy came into work. Stopping on the Forensic's floor, she signed in and headed to Gemma's lab.

Max found her working on a project in her glass enclosed, sterile lab. Knocking on the glass, Gemma looked up from what she was working on and smiled at her. Coming out of her lab, Gemma asked. "Where's your keeper?" Obviously referring to Murphy.

"Not here yet, thank God." Max replied with a smile. "I came by to find out if you have any more information that might help shed any light on my case before he does arrive."

"Well, with your rapid departure the last time you were here, I never did get a chance for the big reveal," Gemma told her. Walking to her desk, she opened the file and took out two transparencies. Sliding them side by side on to the light box, she turned on the light, and started explaining the evidence to Max. "This slide is the DNA of Mr. Lewis and this is the DNA of the fetus," Gemma explained.

"This is what you showed to me the last time," Max stated. "And you said Mr. Lewis was the father, right?"

"No, that's not what I said. I said that Mr. Lewis was related to the fetus." She then took the slides and place them on top of each other. Looking at the two of them on the light box, she could see they had similarities in some areas but completely different in others.

Gemma explained, " There should be twelve to fifteen similar markers if he was the father, but only eight are showing. So Mr. Lewis is related to, but not the father."

"What?" Max exclaimed.

"Science doesn't lie. Either Mr. Lewis had a brother or a son who fathered the baby," Gemma informed her.

Max was so stunned, she was speechless. Finally regaining her senses, she told Gemma, " I don't know if he had a brother, but I do know he had a son and the son was pretty close in age to the mother-in-law."

"I think you're going to have to have a little discussion with the him. I did a quick background check on Mr. Lewis, and I can tell you for sure, that he was an only child, and both of his parents are deceased. So I guess that narrows it down to only one person, the son," Gemma explained.

Max had to agree with Gemma's assessment and realized that this information changed the whole line of questioning for when she re-interviews Ross Lewis again. "Anything else?" she asked.

Gemma pulled another piece of paper from the folder, looked it over, and told Max.

" Our testing of the wounds on the victims, as to the type of weapon used, has proven inconclusive. So I'm sorry, none of our testing seems to match the wound patterns found on the victims. I hate to say it but the type of weapon used still cannot be determined."

"What other alternative do we have?" Max asked, exasperated at her findings.

"I would like to examine the actual tissue of the wound. I'm hoping that perhaps there might be clues found in it." Gemma stated.

"What do you need?" Max her asked.

"I need Ms. Lewis' body for a full forensic examination." Gemma told her. " Which means you or Murphy are going have to request it from the coroner."

Max quickly realized she and Murphy had to get to the coroner's office, make the request and then interview Ross Lewis again. She hoped that she could split the chores, Murphy handling the Coroner's office and her interviewing Ross Lewis.

Thanking Gemma, Max headed up to the top floor to find Murphy. She hoped he was agreeable to splitting up the work load.

Finding Murphy in the break room drinking coffee, she sat down beside him at his table. Explaining what forensic had found, she broached the possibility of splitting up the investigation. He was not in an agreeable mood. "Hell no, we're not splitting anything. We need to get over to Doctor Death before he releases the body, and we can both interview the boy after we're done with that." he told her. Max just rolled her eyes in frustration. *Par for the case,* she thought, realizing that the old Murphy was back.

Exasperated, Max explained that she already had an appointment to talk with Ross Lewis later in the day, so if the had to see the coroner, that they should do it first.

"Well let's get going," Murphy said as he downed the last of his coffee. Max just shook her head as the two of them headed toward the elevator. The ride to the coroner's office was made in silence. Arriving. Murphy told Max, "Let me do the talking again, since I know him." Max just nodded in acquiescence.

Walking down the hallway, past all the gurneys loaded with covered bodies waiting for autopsy, Max though it smelled even worse than it did during the last visit. Passing the last one, she almost gagged because of the smell. She had to put her sleeve over her mouth and nose as she passed it. "That one certainly is ripe," Murphy quipped. Max didn't say anything because the smell was so bad, she didn't want to take a breath to respond.

Walking into the autopsy room, Max thought it appeared worse than the first time she was there. Doctor Deitrich was doing a craniotomy on a body laying on a stainless steel table. He was in the process of extracting the corpse's brain when he noticed Murphy and Max walking in. Placing the brain in a tray placed on the autopsy table, he took off his gloves and walked over to them. Briefly shaking Murphy's hand, he quickly moved to Max. As he took her hand, Max thought his hand was so cold, like that of one of the bodies he worked on.

"It's so nice to see you again, lovely lady. It's Maxine, right?" He stated, staring her in the eyes.

Rather than let Max respond, Murphy interjected, "Yeah, her name is Maxine, but we have other things more pressing than formal niceties. We need you to send Mary Lewis over to our forensic people as quick as possible." he told him caustically.

Max could tell from the look on Doctor Deitrich's face, that Murphy had ruffled his feathers. Continuing to hold Max's hand, he told Murphy, "Well, that might be a little difficult. The body is scheduled for release to the family this afternoon."

" Isn't there some way to delay the release?" Murphy questioned.

"Yes, you could go to the county courthouse and get a judge to sign a stay, or...."

"Or what?" Murphy asked, knowing full well it would be almost impossible to find a judge on a Friday morning.

Still holding Max's hand, Doctor Deitrich told Murphy, " I could accidentally misplace her body for a couple of days, but you know how it works. Quid pro quo. I do you a favor, then you do me a favor."

With that statement, Max felt a sudden sickly feeling churning in her stomach.

"What do you need?" Murphy asked.

"Well," Deitrich said, looking at Max, "There is a major Hollywood movie premier tonight. I have two tickets for the formal opening, and my date has unexpectedly come down with something, so I need a stand-in date."

With that statement, Murphy and Deitrich looked directly at Max. Max had a sinking feeling in her stomach and it wasn't from the smell in the room. All the blood ran from her head as she tried to not to have a look of panic on her face. A long moment of silence followed.

" I'm sure that Detective Somers would be happy to act as your date for the evening. Right detective?" Murphy stated, breaking the silence.

Max was in a quandary trying to decide what to say. Finally, she realized that she had no options. "Sure," she replied, continuing. "Just how formal is this thing?"

"Red carpet formal with lots of paparazzi and big name stars," Deitrich explained.

"Just to let you know, I paid a lot of money for these premier tickets and it's been a tradition for me to walk the red carpet when I attend, and I fully expect to continue to do so," Deitrich informed her. Max's stomach started churning even more. She almost thought she could vomit.

Deitrich saw the look an Max's face. " Don't worry my Dear. If you accept, you're just going to be my arm candy. I'm sure that when the evening is over, your virginity will still be intact." he solemnly told her.

Max had to smile at his comment and started to feel a little more relaxed. "I don't think I have to worry about that. After two husbands and a grown daughter, that ship has sailed a long time ago," she replied to him.

A smile came to Deitrich face with her comment. " Well spoken, my dear. I think we will have a very interesting evening. Very interesting indeed. If you give me your address, I will have my town car pick you up at seven. Dinner first and then the premier at nine. Think you can be ready by then?" Deitrich asked.

"Sure, seven will be fine, " she told him. Max then wrote her address on the back of one of her business card and handed it to him.

Taking the card, he told her, "I will see you at seven then, and please, my friends call me Emil." He took her hand again and gave it a formal kiss.

"You'll transfer Mrs. Lewis over to Forensics today?" she asked him, her stomach slowly settling down.

"Consider it done," he assured her. " I'll personally handle the transfer and if anybody asks, we have temporarily misplaced her body."

"Thanks Emil," Murphy stated to him.

Deitrich gave Murphy a look of disdain, "The lovely lady can call me Emil, you call me Dr. Deitrich," he explained to Murphy. This brought a smile to Max's face. Seeing her smile, Deitrich smiled back at her and escorted her to the door. "Bring you appetite, my dear. And please relax and enjoy yourself tonight. I promise I won't bite," he told her with a warm smile. Then looking at Murphy he continued, "But him, I won't promise."

As Max and Murphy left the county coroner's office, they walked in silence. Getting into the car, Murphy broke the silence. "Well, that went well, didn't it,"

Max sat in the car, seething on the inside. "Yeah, real well, partner," Max addressed him, with heavy sarcasm on the word 'partner'.

"What do you mean by that?" Murphy questioned.

" You threw me under the bus, you jerk. I could have cajoled Deitrich to transfer the body without having to go out with him. But no, you had to open your big mouth and volunteer me to be, what did he call me, arm candy?" she almost screamed at him.

"Okay, okay, but it worked, didn't it?" Murphy rebutted.

" Oh, just shut up you chauvinistic jerk. I'm sure I could have talked him into transferring the body with out having to out on a date with him. Now start the car and drive to UCLA before I really hurt you," she threatened. The trip to the campus, thankfully for Max, was in relative silence. Arriving at the campus building that housed the research lab, it only took a few minutes to find Ross. He was about to take a break in the building's lunch room, so Max asked if they could accompany him as they had a few additional questions for him.. As they walked toward the break room, Ross asked, "How is the investigation going? Any good clues into who killed my dad?"

Murphy was about to answer, but Max gave him a look that caused him to keep his mouth shut. Arriving at the break area, Ross poured himself a cup of coffee and sat at a empty table. Since most of the break room was empty, he picked a spot that was away from the few other people that were in the room. Max and Murphy joined him.

"How can I help you, Officers?" he questioned as he stirred his coffee, trying to cool it down.

Max started. " I know your feelings toward your step mother, but how do you feel about your sister?"

Ross was taken aback by the question. " I love my sister. I would do anything for her. Why would you ask that question?"

"Well we found her diary hidden in her bedroom, and she seems to have a lot of anger directed at you written in it. When we questioned her about it, she said it was because you had left the house for collage, leaving her all alone with your step mother." Max questioned.

Ross quickly replied, "Makes sense, I know she didn't get along with her either, so she probably harbors some resentment at me for leaving her alone there at the house. Is there any thing else you need to know?"

"Well now that you mention it, did you know your step mother was pregnant?" Max asked.

"No, no way." He said, visibly shaken. "I'm pretty sure my dad had a vasectomy over ten years ago, so there's no way she could be pregnant, unless?" He trailed off,

"Unless she was having an affair, right?" Max questioned.

Ross immediately turned red and responded, "Right." Crumpling up his coffee cup and pitching it into the trash. " Perhaps he had a vasectomy reversal for his new wife? She had him so wrapped around her finger, he would probably do something like that for her," he suggested. Rising from the table, he added. " Look, I need to get back to work. Anything else?"

"No, I think that just about covers everything. Officer Murphy, do you have any questions?" Max asked.

Murphy rubbed his chin in calm contemplation, and responded, "No, I think that just about covers everything for me. Thank you for your time."

Max was surprised at Murphy's demeanor as he thanked Ross too.

"If you need anything else, next time please set up an appointment," Ross informed them as he walked away.

Once he was gone, Murphy asked, "What did you think?"

"Lying like hell," Max replied. "What about you?"

"Same thought." Murphy concurred, then asked her "Have you got an evidence bag on you?" He asked as he reached into his pocket and pulled out a pair of latex gloves. He then slowly walked over to the trash bin.

"I don't leave home without one." Max assured him, pulling a bag out of her back pocket. She instinctively knew what Murphy was planning, and put on a pair of gloves for herself.

Murphy took an ink pen out of his pocket and proceeded to hook Ross's crumpled up coffee cup on it. Securing it, he walked over to Max who was holding the evidence bag open and proceeded to drop it in. Max sealed the bag, then asked Murphy, " I thought you didn't trust forensics?"

All Murphy said was, "Old dog- new tricks," with a sly smile.

# Chapter 11

Arriving back at the precinct, Murphy informed Max he was going to catch a late lunch at Mike's Bar and she should drop off the new evidence at Forensics. Max gave him a dirty look as she pushed the elevator button for the Forensic floor.

"And don't forget to check if they got the body from the coroner's office and make sure you're all gussied up for your date tonight." This last comment by Murphy really drew a scowl on Max's face. She didn't see the smirk on Murphy's face as he headed off to Mike's Bar.

Max was fuming in the elevator all the way up to Forensics. Arriving at the floor, she took Ross's used coffee cup to Forensics for testing. Gemma wasn't there to receive it but her assistant, Phil was. After getting the cup logged in, she asked him if Mary Lewis's body had arrived.

The assistant confirmed that it did and that a note had accompanied the body addressed to her. Opening the envelope, it read, 'Maxine- I'm sorry for pressuring you into going to the movie premier, but I promise you will have a wonderful evening. So please relax and enjoy your self tonight. See you at seven. Emil.'

After reading the note, she started feeling a little more relaxed about what was about to transpire that evening. Putting the note back in it's envelope, she placed it in her pocket. Thanking Phil, she asked him if Gemma would be in the next day. Phil explained that she was on call for the weekend so it was entirely possible.

"Could you leave her a message to call me if she comes in to work? She has my phone number. Tell her any time is convenient." Max requested.

"Sure will. Are you coming in to work tomorrow?" Phil asked.

"Yes," she responded, continuing, "I'm under a dead line to solve this case and I'm pretty sure, barring a miracle, I'm not going to make it. So yes, I too, will be working this weekend."

"O'Neil on your case?" Phil questioned.

"Not yet but I'm sure I'm on his short list after my melt down in the office the other day," she told him.

"That was you?" He asked.

"Yes, that was me." Max replied, knowing it wasn't her finest moment.

"Well good for you. It's about time somebody took Murphy down a peg or two. Don't worry, just about everyone here wants to tell Murphy what an ass he is. You just did it. Way to go, girl." Phil told her in a congratulatory way.

Well it didn't seem to make my point with Murphy, He's still the same old jerk," Max stated.

"At least you tried. Anyway, I'll give Gemma your message," Phil told her.

Max nodded her head in acknowledgement, and told him thanks, then took the elevator up to the office.

Arriving at the top floor, she went looking for Frank. Finding him at his desk, She updated him about what she and Murphy had discovered over the last two days. She knew their progress would be reported directly to his boss. She told him she was hoping that maybe O'Brien might give her and Murphy a couple of extra days on his deadline. She didn't feel that she had to inform him about her 'date' that evening, even though she felt it was work related.

Frank congratulated her on the progress shown and told her he would convey the case's progress to O'Brien and hopefully get her a couple of more days to solve it.

"Do you think he'll extend it?" Max asked plaintively.

"Don't know until I ask. Are you coming in tomorrow?" Frank asked.

"Yeah, I have an obligation tonight, but I need some answers from Forensics that might be the break we need," Max explained to him.

"We?" Frank asked.

"Murphy is actually cooperating on the case, and is now a firm believer in forensics," Max explained.

Frank was speechless for a few seconds. "Murphy is cooperating and using forensics? That's a first," he said feigning astonishment. All Max could do was smile. "You'll see. I think he's coming around. He even got me a date for tonight," Max told him with a forced smile, deciding it probably be best that she told him the details about the quid pro quo deal with Deitrich.

"He got you a date? With who?" Frank asked.

"Emil Deitrich," Max told him.

"Wait, I know that name from somewhere," Frank paused in contemplation, then recognition came over his face. "Wait-isn't he the…"

"The head county coroner," Max finished the sentence for him, blushing a little.

"Oh wow!" Frank exclaimed, continuing, "He's a pretty big person in the society pages," he told Max. "Where is he taking you?"

"His girl friend is sick or something, so I'm filling in for her for some movie premier tonight," she explained.

"And Murphy set this up for you?" Frank asked.

"Yup," was all Max said.

"Better watch yourself. If Murphy is involved. Be very careful," Frank warned her.

"Don't worry. It's kind of a quid pro quo arrangement," Max explained, not filling in the details of what the quid or the quo entailed.

"Well, you have fun and be prepared to tell me all about the details tomorrow," he commanded.

"You'll be here tomorrow?" Max questioned.

"Yea, I have a bunch of paper work to catch up on, so I'll see you sometime tomorrow," Frank explained.

"Okay then. I need to get home and prepare for my big date tonight. I'll see you tomorrow, when I get here," she told him as she headed for the elevator.

"Have fun," Frank yelled at her as she stepped into the waiting elevator.

Arriving back at her apartment, she saw there were several messages on her answering machine. She realized there wasn't enough time to answer them or even check them out, but resolved to deal with them first thing in the morning.

She found her little black dress way in the back of her closet and a pair of high heels that went with it. After taking a shower, she fixed her hair and put on some make up, then put on her dress, praying it still fit her. It did.

Looking at herself in the mirror, she thought to herself. *Not too bad for a thirty five year old police detective.*

Sitting on the edge of her bed, she loaded her matching clutch purse with the needed supplies she might need for the evening, and took a few minutes just to relax. It had been a hectic day for her and she needed the time to unwind.

She sat there for several minutes, trying to catch her breath, until she heard the buzzer ringing, notifying her that someone had arrived at the ground level door for her.

"Emil?" she spoke into the intercom.

"No ma'am. I'm Spike, your chauffeur. Mr. Deitrich is waiting for you in the limo," a voice answered back to her.

Max was both irritated and yet impressed. Irritated at being called 'ma'am, a term she hated being called, and impressed that there was a limo waiting for her. This would be her first time riding in a limousine, an experience she never thought she would ever experience. Walking downstairs to the front door, she saw a huge man who could have passed for a professional football player, dressed in a black suit and tie. Holding the apartment building door open for her, he escorted her to the white stretch limo waiting for her at the curb. Opening limo the door for her, she stepped inside the vehicle and found Emil waiting for her.

"Good evening, Detective. You look lovely this evening. I'm sure if you were to interrogate your suspects looking like you do, they would confess in a heartbeat." Deitrich complemented to her. Max gave him a polite thank you.

The drive to dinner took them to a five star restaurant. Arriving at the restaurant, the limo driver pulled under an overhead canopy. Stopping, both back doors of the limo were immediately opened by waiting doormen. Exiting the limo, another doorman opened the restaurant's front door. Waiting for them was the maitre d', who ushered them them to their reserved table.

Emil was slightly disappointed when he found out that Max didn't drink, but they both enjoyed a marvelous meal. Emil was a great conversationalist and made Max feel comfortable even when several people stopped by their table to say hello. Emil introduced Max to all who stopped and all were amazed that she was a police detective. By the end of the meal, Max was feeling relaxed and started having a good time.

After the meal was over, Emil checked his watch and stated that they needed to get going to the premier. He signaled for the meitre d' who came to their table immediately. Emil asked for him to have the limo brought to the front door. He complied immediately, so by the time they were outside, the limo was waiting for them.

"I take it you're not a stranger to the staff here," Max stated, as the limo pulled away from the restaurant.

"You would be correct in that assumption." he replied, "Jennie, my girl friend and I come here about once a week, so yes, I'm no stranger."

"I hope I'm not getting you in any trouble with her," Max inquired.

"No, you're not," he responded. "But I'm afraid I haven't been entirely honest with you." With that news, Max's stomach started to tighten up a little with the statement, and she started to feel nervous again.

Emil noticed the change in her demeanor and explained to her. "My Jennie isn't sick. She is nine months pregnant and is ready to deliver any day now. It was she who insisted I find a substitute for tonight so as to get me out of the house. She said I was driving her crazy."

With his explanation, Max felt more at ease again, and told him, " Congratulations, do you know if it's a boy or girl?" Max asked.

"Don't know and don't care. Just want it healthy," Emil stated to her.

With that statement, Max began to really relax and sat back on the leather limo seat and enjoyed the ride to the theater for the premier.

After about ten minutes in the limo, Emil broke the silence. "We're almost to the theater, so if you need to check your makeup or anything, now is the time to do it. When we get there, you'll be in the center of a whirlwind of paparazzi as we walk the red carpet."

Max felt nervous again, this time for a different reason. "Do we have to go in the front? Can't we just sneak in the back door?" She asked, half- heartidly.

"I'm sorry, my dear, but the red carpet is the most fun part of the whole evening. Now when we get to the theater and exit the limo, you'll take my arm and I will guide you to the spot where we stop and you strike a Hollywood pose. Count to ten and then follow me into the theater. Don't speak to any reporters, either." Emil explained to her.

"Hollywood pose? What is a Hollywood pose?" Max questioned him.

"Where the hell have you been, girl? Haven't you seen these movie premiers before on television?" He asked.

"No, I don't watch much television, and the news just depresses me" she replied, becoming slightly exasperated.

" It's just my luck to be with the one woman in Los Angeles who doesn't watch television," Emil replied with a smile, continuing, "Okay, when we are stopped on the red carpet, let go of my arm, place both hands on your hips, make a quarter turn toward me and then turn you head to face the cameras. Oh, and by the way, tip your head back a tad and try give a sultry look."

Max had a puzzled look on her face. Emil read it and then told her, "Look- pretend our driver is me and I am you," he said, as he sat forward in the seat, put his hands on his hips and emulated the pose he had described to her. Max couldn't help but giggle at what she saw. The limo driver also started snickering. Emil took their reactions good naturedly, then asked her, " Do you want to practice before we get there?"

Max compliantly sat forward in the car seat and copied what Emil had demonstrated. "Perfect, but don't forget the sultry look," he stated to her. She tried a second time. "Fantastic, well done" Emil told her.

Max felt a little uncomfortable but was determined to get through the charade. Arriving at the theater, they were immediately whisked onto the red carpet. True to his word, Emil and Max slowly walked to the spot and stopped. Max did her best on her Hollywood pose. The paparazzi cameras exploded in her face, temporarily blinding her. Thankfully, Emil took her by the arm and guided her into the theater.

After the movie, a detective thriller, Emil led her back to the front of the theater were there were a small crowd of fans hoping for an autograph from some of the stars attending the premier. Fortunately for Max, the fans weren't interested in the county coroner and his date.

Getting into the limo, the driver drove them quickly away from the theater. After a minute or two, Emil asked if Max wanted to stop some where for a non-alcoholic night cap. Max declined, telling him that she had to get up early to work on her case. Emil understood and ordered the driver to drive to Max's address. Dropping her off, he told her, "Thank you for your company. I hope you had an enjoyable evening. You were a tremendously good sport about it all."

Max thanked him and told him that the evening was indeed 'Interesting,' and congratulated him on his future fatherhood.

Max watch the taillights of the limo fade down the street. Taking a deep breath, she had to admit that the evening truly was most interesting, but she was very glad it was over. She had kept her promise and now could get back to her case.

Putting the code into the keypad by the front door, she took the elevator up to her apartment. Entering her darkened apartment, she started to close the door when suddenly she felt someone from behind, grab her hair, forcing her head back and then she felt a knife blade on her throat.

# Chapter 12

Max's police training kicked in as she easily disarmed the person behind her. To her astonishment, the person holding the knife was her next door neighbor, Pam.

"What are you doing here, Pam? I thought you were still at the halfway house," Max asked incredulously.

"I was but I got kicked out," Pam stated.

"You started using again," Max stated.

"Yeah," Pam sheepishly confirmed.

"Why? It's only been a couple of days. You were doing so good," Max questioned.

"I don't know. I guess I just got depressed and needed a fix. I miss Sammy so much. I really need him back," she replied plaintively.

"And the fighting and bruises? You miss that too?" Max countered. Exasperation sounding in her voice.

" I know, I know. Look, I know he's not perfect, but he says he loves me when we're not fighting." Pam told her.

" I know he told you that, and I told you I would find him, so why the breaking and entering and the knife to my throat?" Max questioned.

A sly smile crept across Pam's face. "Technically, I didn't break in. I talked the landlord into letting me in, and I did hold the dull side of the knife to your throat, not the sharp blade. I really am sorry about that, but I wasn't sure how you would react, finding me in your apartment and besides, I did not want to get shot. But I see from the way you're dressed, I guess you have no place to hide a gun," Pam explained, looking at Max dressed in her evening attire.

Max recognized the validity of Pam's argument, and although upset with her, she was upset more about the landlord opening the door of her apartment for Pam. She resolved it was time to find another place to live.

Turning her attention back to Pam, she told her, "I think I know what happened to Sammy but I need another day or two to find him. I need you to have patience. Can you do that for me?"

Pam was silent for a couple of moments then responded. "Okay, I can give you that. But you have to promise you'll find him for me."

Max immediately told her, "I promise you, but now we have to deal with your situation. You know I should arrest you for that stunt you pulled with the knife, but I will overlook it for now. I think it's too late to get you back to the halfway house, so I'm going to ask you to go back to your apartment and stay there. Don't go out, don't call anybody, and most importantly, don't start using again. Okay?"

Pam immediately seemed to brighten up with what Max told her, and promised her to do everything Max told her. Max opened her apartment door, signaling that Pam had to leave. As Pam departed, she turned and stated, "You promise to find him."

"I promise," Max said, reassuring her.

After Pam left, Max wondered to herself if she had done the right thing. She finally realized that the dice were cast and that there was no going back. A promise is a promise.

She had a restless night, tossing and turning, trying to get a handle on her murder cases. The next morning she checked on Pam and re-enforced what she had told her the night before. Making sure Pam understood that she stay in her apartment, Max left for work. Arriving at the precinct, she noticed she was almost the first one there for her Saturday shift. She was hoping for Frank to be there but he appeared to have not arrived yet. Sitting at her desk, she proceeded to turn on her computer and check her messages. One of the first messages she saw was from Gemma in Forensics, telling her she had to see Max as soon as she got the message.

Max felt a glimmer of hope that there might be a break in her case. As she headed for the elevator, she ran into Frank as he was arriving to work. "How was the evening?" He asked, as Max passed him.

"Tell you all about it when I get back. Got to go to Forensics," she told him, getting into the elevator.

Arriving at Forensics, she quickly found Gemma. When Gemma saw Max, she immediately walked over to her. "Good news?" Max asked her.

"Yes and no," Gemma told Max.

"Let me have it," Max asked.

"Well, it was a quiet Friday night, so Phil had nothing to do but work on your case and play with some new software we are trying out." Gemma told her.

"Great, what did he discover with the new software?" Max asked,hopefully.

"Well, lets start with your nurse who was wearing the men's shoes. We ran what we could see of the face on the video through a facial recognition program and found no matches as far as previous offenders in our data base, but when he ran it through the general population data base, he found a match that was eighty two percent probability as far as being your person." Gemma announced. Max started to feel that possibly the case was about to break wide open. She knew though an eighty two percent match would never hold up in court, but at least it was finally a firm lead.

"Okay, who is it?" Max asked.

"Just wait. There's more. Phil ran the DNA off of your coffee cup and you have a positive match for the paternity of the fetus." Gemma told her.

"One hundred per cent match?" Max exclaimed.

"Ninety nine point eight percent match. Close enough for evidence in court," Gemma confidently told her.

Max was stunned. She realized the implications of the DNA match. It meant that Ross Lewis was the father of his stepmother's baby.

"Wait, what about the identification of the fake nurse." Max asked.

Gemma pulled out two photo's out of a file folder and showed them to Max. The first photo was a close up of the nurse in the video, showing the forehead, eyes and cheeks in detail.

The second photo was of another person whose lower face had been blocked off so only the same details of the face were shown.

"Where did you get the second photo?" Max inquired. Her excitement building.

"It came from the UCLA student identification web site," she told Max. She then showed her an unblocked photo of the same person. It was Ross Lewis. " The computer analysis confirms an eighty two percent match between your fake nurse and Ross Lewis," Gemma told her confidently.

All Max could do was stand there dumbfounded, at complete loss for words. The implication of the evidence overwhelming to her. Not only did Ross father Mary Lewis' baby but probably killed her in the hospital. Max knew there was no way to explain away the DNA evidence, but how could she prove that Ross was the fake nurse.

But the larger question was who shot Mary Lewis and the other victims in the first place. She knew that Ross had an airtight alibi for the carnage at the mansion, so he was probably not involved in that crime, unless he hired someone else to carry it out.. What ever the circumstances, Max knew it was time to pull Ross in for a formal interrogation and conduct a thorough search of his residence and work location.

"Anything else found that might help?" Max asked.

Gemma just frowned and shook her head, then told her, " Mrs. Lewis died from an air embolism in the heart, caused by an injection of air through her IV line. However, the initial wound in the her back was caused by an unknown projectile. The strange part is, a bullet would cause tearing and ripping of the flesh and thus cause severe hemorrhaging of arteries and veins. This didn't happen with Mrs. Lewis but did happen with the other three victims. Those victims bled out almost immediately, but Mary Lewis didn't, and I don't know why.

And last, but most strange, there was an abnormal level of nitrogen saturation in the tissue and blood cells around her wound's entry point."

"Which means?" Max asked.

"I don't know," Gemma told her. "I got the questions. You need to find the answers," she told Max.

Gemma's information felt like a blow to the stomach for Max. She felt that she had more information to work with but nothing that would lead to a resolution of her case. Thanking Gemma, she headed back upstairs to talk to Frank. It took a couple of minutes to find him in his office. He gave her a big smile once he saw her heading toward his desk. Grabbing a chair for her to sit on and placing it close to his, he kept smiling the entire time it took for Max to arrive. Sitting down in the provided chair, Frank asked her, in a soap opera whisper, "Well, how did it go last night? Don't leave anything out. Tell me everything." he demanded.

Max reluctantly told him the details from the previous evening, excluding the details of her assault by Pam. Frank just kept broadly smiling during her whole description of the evening that Max was giving him. Finally finishing, Max couldn't hide her curiosity any more and asked, "What is so funny? Why the silly grin?"

Frank opened his desk drawer and brought out a newspaper. "Obviously you haven't seen the social section of the morning newspaper yet." he told her as he opened up the Saturday morning paper to the society page.

Max stared at the paper, seeing photos from the movie premier she had attended the night before. The first five photos were of some of the stars and the movers and shakers of

Hollywood walking the red carpet, then the sixth one, someone had circled in a red magic marker, was a photo of her and Emil on the red carpet. *Oh my God,* she thought to her self as she read the caption on the bottom of the photo. There, in print, was her name in black and white, 'Dr. Emil Deitrich, County Coroner and Beverly Hills Detective, Maxine Somers, enjoying a night on the red carpet,' the caption read. There she was, doing the pose that Emil taught her. Her face immediately turned beet red.

Frank saw her reaction and told her, "Looking hot, girl. You clean up pretty good."

Max knew he meant it as a compliment, but she was still embarrassed. "Thanks," she replied with a squeak, feeling hot all over. "Please don't show that to anybody here," she pleaded to him.

Frank just kept smiling and told her, "I won't, but do you know how many others here in this building read the same paper. All it's going to take is one person, and then everybody will see it. You're not going to be able to hide it for too long. You do know that, right?"

Max knew he was right. The only alternative was to buck up and take any good- natured ribbing that her co- workers might give her.

"I don't suppose I could steal all the newspapers around here before they get read?" she asked good- naturedly.

"No, I don't think that would work," Frank replied with a smile, continuing, "Look, you really look good in the picture, and you had a great time, didn't you? You'll probably never have to do that again and you got a great story to tell your daughter and grand kids someday."

Max new he was right and decided to face all the ribbing she knew was coming.

"Look, at lunch time, bring you and your lunch over here and tell me all about your evening," Frank requested.

"Okay, that sounds good. I'll see you then," Max told him. As she started to walk away, she turned and gave Frank her red carpet pose. Frank was just taking a sip of coffee as she did it, and immediately choked and almost spilled the coffee over the top of his desk, trying to hold back his laughter. "Thanks, buddy," he told Max as he tried to clean the mess on his desk up with tissues.

"See you at lunch," was all she said as she walked away.

Heading to her cubicle, she knew Murphy wouldn't be in that day, and decided to start the paperwork needed to get a search warrant for Ross Lewis' work and residence. After she finished the paperwork and sent it to District Attorney for processing, she started making a list of questions she planned to ask him. She knew that he wasn't aware of what new information she had, so she thought some how she'd try to phrase her questions in such a way so that he might incriminate himself. She also knew she was running out of time. She hoped she could trap him into admitting to the murder of Mary Lewis at the hospital quickly. She hoped that maybe with a confession, she might get some extra time from O'Brien to solve the other three murders.

*If wishes were horses, then a beggar would ride,* she thought to herself. Her father, when he was still alive, had always told her this adage when she was small girl, but she never fully understood the implications of the saying until just now.

Finishing up her list of questions for Ross, she looked at her watch and realized it was getting close to lunch time. Going to the refrigerator in the break room, she retrieved her lunch and hit the soda machine for a soft drink, then headed to Franks desk. Frank was buried in a stack of files that he was slowly processing through.

"Looks like you're ready for a break," Max told him.

Looking up from his stack of files, he smiled at her and said, "Thank you, I really do need a break. You showed up at just the right time."

"Looks like you've got a couple of days of work there," Max told him.

"That and more," Frank told her, as he cleared a space on his desk for their lunches. Taking a sandwich, a bag of chips and a bottle of water out of his side desk drawer, he indicated to Max to use the cleared space on his desk for her lunch. Max settled in to the space he offered.

"What are you working on?" she asked as she started eating her lunch.

"Transfer files for the last three months. I hate doing them but it's part of the job," he explained.

Suddenly, Max thought there might be a way for Frank and his files to solve the disappearance of Sonny O'Brien.

"Are these files available to the general public or are they confidential?" Max asked him as she formulated a plan in her mind.

"Nah, anybody with a valid reason like a relative or the press can access them online. Why?" Frank replied.

"Looking for a missing prisoner that was in lock-up a few days ago but seems to have disappeared from the booking records. Would he be in your files?" She asked.

"All bookings have a log-in record and a transfer file. If your prisoner was in the jail, then there should be a file here," he told Max, pointing at the stack of files on his desk.

"How are the files arranged," Max asked.

"Alphabetically," Frank responded, continuing, "Do you have a last name?"

"O'Brien, Sammy O'Brien," Max told him, almost in a whisper.

"What?" Frank responded with astonishment, "The chief's son? You got to be kidding me."

"You heard me right, and I'm not kidding," Max told him,

Immediately Frank started going through the stack of files on his desk, finally pulling one of the files out of the stack. Opening it up, he started flipping through the paper work that was in it.

"You're right. Here is his booking photo and the charges. Possession with intent to distribute. The report says he had a kilo of crack cocaine in his possession and almost three thousand dollars in cash. He also resisted arrest," he told Max, astonished.

"Does it say where he is now?" Max asked, continuing, "He should be in Central, awaiting his arraignment. Right?"

Frank flipped through the pages again, and then informed her, " He should be but he's not. It says here in the file, he was transferred to LCRP."

"What the hell is LCRP?" Max asked.

"Last Chance Recovery Program. That's basically a restricted recovery program for the rich and famous, or high priority snitches," Frank explained. "It's like a lock up at a fancy hotel.

" Is that normal?" Max questioned.

"No, someone pulled some very heavy strings to get this accomplished," he told her.

"Like Chief O'Brien?" Max asked,

"Yeah, like Chief O'Brien, but I can't believe he'd do such a thing. It's totally against policy. He could really get into a lot of trouble," Frank told her plaintively.

"Even for his son?" Max asked.

"Yeah, even for his son." Frank replied.

"What are you going to do?" she asked him.

"I don't know. I guess nothing for right now, but I'm going to have to do something eventually. I can't let something like this slide. Max, you really opened up a can of worms, with this information." Frank informed her.

"Am I in trouble?" She asked him.

"Of course not. You did the right thing. The only problem might be that O'Brien has a lot of friends in high places. You might not be real popular with some of his buddies after this hit's the fan, but that's their problem, not yours."

"Great, I've been a detective for a little over a week, and I'm already making enemies in the department," Max told him, half jokingly.

"Well, welcome to the club," Frank told her, continuing, "In case you didn't notice, my title here is Assistant Deputy Chief, but in reality, I'm nothing more than a glorified office boy with a title, working in beautiful down town Beverly Hills."

"What did you do?" Max questioned.

"I got married to my partner," he explained to her, continuing, "When O'Brien found out, my career was basically over. My partner was transferred to beach patrol at Venice Beach, and I was promoted here, just for the optics. I should have been promoted to Chief a couple of years ago, but here I am, still just Chief Office Manager."

"Why don't you complain to your union rep?" She asked.

"Look Max, I got eighteen years in, with two more to go. Once I got in my twenty years, Robert and I are out of here and retiring to some island in the Pacific," Frank informed her, " The last thing I'm going to do is poke the bear and screw everything up," he explained to her.

"I can understand that, but isn't reporting what O'Brien did, poking the bear?" Max asked.

"Oh I'm not going to report him. I'll just let someone else turn him in. All I have to do is subtly provide the evidence to the people who I report to at Central. I'll let them figure it out." Frank told her.

"And if it doesn't work?" Max inquired.

"I'll just bide my time and wait. One good thing about the police department, they keep real good records and they never throw anything out. If need be, I'll just wait until my last day on the job and then drop the dime on O'Brien," he told Max, continuing, " I got a few other tidbits of policy infractions that, by them selves seem minor, but taken all together, looks pretty serious."

"Well I hope your plan works. In the meantime, I now know where his son disappeared to. I can tell his girl friend that I found him and that he is safe but unavailable for awhile. I just wished I could solve my murder case a easy as this," Max told him.

"Don't worry. Look at how far you've come," Frank reassured her.

Max knew he was right, but she also new that she was running out of time.

"Let's finish our lunches. I'm sorry if I side tracked you?" Max told her apologetically.

"No problem." Frank told her. " I'm just glad to help."

Max and Frank finished eating and spent a while talking about her case. Max told him about her frustration with Murphy and what evidence they had discovered.

"Looks like you and Murphy have made great strides in your case. Just keep following the leads and you'll break the case. It just takes time," Frank counseled her.

"I know you're right but it seems time is something we don't have. O'Brien wants this case off the books within two more days. I'd like to tell him that he's being unreasonable with what evidence there is to work with, because I don't want to look inadequate or incompetent to him on my first case," she lamented.

Frank contemplated her comments then replied to her, "Look, Murphy is a seasoned detective and has solved some pretty difficult cases. If he can't put this case to bed, then probably no one can. So please, don't beat yourself up. Some cases never do get solved," Frank advised her.

Max knew that he was right but she was still determined to solve her first case. "I know what you're saying is true, but I just have this nagging feeling in the back of my mind that I'm missing something important. It's bugging me to distraction trying to figure out what it is," Max told him.

"I'm sure you'll figure it out. About the only thing I think you might try is to pull an incident report on the address of the house. There might be a clue found there," Frank volunteered to her.

"That's a great idea. Can I do it on my computer?" Max asked.

Frank grabbed a piece of paper from his desk and wrote a computer address on it. He then wrote down a series of numbers on the paper. "Here's the county computer web site and the pass code to access that information you need. You'll probably use it a lot in some of your other cases, so you might want to save it." he advised.

Max thanked him profusely as she took the paper from him. Cleaning up the remains of her lunch, she went back to her cubicle and logged on to her computer, inputting the information that Frank had given her. Once she was on the web page, it asked for her name, rank and badge number. After entering the required identifying information, the site asked for the address of the location. Max had to get out her notebook to verify the address, inputted it into the computer, and waited for any results.

She was astonished when the report flashed up on the computer screen. She saw more than twenty incident reports fill up her computer screen. Some of them going back over seven years ago. *These go way back to wife number one,* Max thought to herself.

Looking at the reports of the responding officers, she could see the history of a dysfunctional family from domestic disturbances to drunk and disorderly and finally to juvenile runaway. The runaways were reported, not once but three times, along with multiple calls for excessive noise.

*I guess this family isn't exactly a typical Beverly Hills stereotype,* Max thought to herself. With this new information, she realized that she and Murphy needed to talk to the the first wife. She was the only person in the family they hadn't interviewed yet, if they could. First though, she knew that she had to procure the search warrant for Ross Lewis' property.

But before that, Max decided to call Pam and give her the good news as far locating Sammy. Dialing Pam up on the telephone, all she heard was the ring tone. Waiting a few minutes, she tried again but with no results.

*Damn it. I told her to stay in her apartment. Where could she be?* Max pondered to herself. I told her to stay in her apartment, *Why didn't she listen to me?*

Hanging up the phone, she decided there wasn't anything more she could do at work, so she informed Frank that she was heading home. "Be safe," he replied to her. "You too." Max told him.

# Chapter 13

Arriving back at her place, Max went over to Pam's apartment and pounded on her door. After trying several more times, she started to feel concerned. Finding the building superintendent, she identified herself and asked if he would open Pam's apartment door.

He was hesitant at first until Max brought up the fact that he had let Pam into her place. Opening the door, Max was hesitant entering, fearing what she might find. Her main concern was if Pam may have got her hands on some drugs and in her depressed state of mind, overdosed due to her addiction.

Entering the apartment, her fears were for nought, as it appeared unoccupied. Calling out to her and hearing no response, she quickly checked out the rest of the apartment. Finding nothing, she had the superintendent re-lock the apartment door. As they were leaving, she instructed him to inform her if he saw Pam or made any contact with him.

Returning to her apartment with some take out food, she turned on the television and watched local the news as she ate supper. The main news story that evening was coverage of a major drug arrest in Beverly Hills. As the reporter on the TV described the details of the bust, the television broadcast the perpetrators as they were marched into the police vans. Although she tried to hide her face with her hands, Max recognized Pam as she was being placed into the police van. Max really wasn't that all surprised.

*Well, I guess I know where Pam is,* Max thought to herself. *Guess I'll be seeing her Monday morning, and then I can tell her where her boyfriend is.*

Max enjoyed her Sunday off, cleaning the apartment, doing some laundry and taking herself out for lunch and dinner. Arriving at work on Monday, as she stepped off of the elevator, she was greeted by a life size cardboard cut out of her taken from the newspaper social page. The effigy was displayed predominately, waiting for her in front of the elevator door.

When the other officers saw her getting off the elevator, they applauded and did some catcall whistle. Max, although slightly embarrassed, took a deep breath and walked up to the effigy, and playfully mimicked same pose as the cutout. As she tried to head for her desk among all the applause and whistles, she saw Frank trying to duck her gaze. It didn't work. As she walked past him, she whispered, " I'll get you back for this, buddy." with a smile on her face. All Frank could do was smile back.

Arriving at her desk, she saw Murphy was back. "Welcome back, partner. How did your day in court go?" she questioned.

"I hate doing court time. I sat there in the court most of the day waiting to testify, and then the defendant pleads guilty before I had a chance to get on the stand. So, basically, a wasted day," he complained.

"Sorry to hear that, but I got a bunch of news for you. Guess who the father was of Mrs. Lewis' baby is, and is also our mystery nurse?" Max asked. Murphy's attitude changed immediately. "Ross Lewis!" He responded.

"Bingo, Ross Lewis. I processed a search warrant Saturday which I hope is going to be ready sometime today. Also, Frank suggested that I run an incident report on the victims address and doing so, I found over twenty police reports going back to wife number one. Something has been bothering me that we were missing. Something important, and that something was interviewing the ex-wife. That is if we can," Max informed him, as she handed him the print out of the incident report.

Murphy took a few moments to look through the report she handed him and told her,

" Good job, rookie. Looks like you've been productive over the weekend."

"Thanks," she replied, "What do you want to do next?"

"Well, I think we need to visit wife number one," Murphy suggested, "and give Ross a visit this afternoon."

" Do Ross this afternoon? What about the search warrant?" She questioned.

"I think that we need a plan. So why don't you give the District Attorney a call and see if the search warrant is ready, and if not find out when it will be," he told her.

"Okay, any thing else?" She asked.

"Yeah, call Ms. Jackson over at Lewis Industries and find out where the first wife has been institutionalized, and then call the place where she is located and make an appointment to see her this morning. I'd call Jackson myself but I think you get along with her better than I do," Murphy told her.

Max gave him a grin, imagining Murphy having a dialogue with Ms. Jackson and then asked, "What will you be doing?"

"O'Brien wants an update on our case and to discuss some other things. It shouldn't take too long to fill him in," Murphy explained, as he headed to the chief's office.

Max proceeded to get on the phone with Ms. Jackson as Murphy went to his meeting with O'Brien. Dialing up the number, she quickly was connected with her. Obtaining the requested information, she then called the District Attorney and found out that the search warrant was ready. She asked that a copy of it be faxed over to her for processing.

After completing her tasks, she called the care facility where the first Mrs. Lewis was institutionalized and made an appointment to interview her for that morning. She then sat back and waited for the warrant to come through. About twenty minutes later, Frank came to her desk with the printed warrant.

"Where's Murphy?" he asked, handing her the warrant.

"O'Brien wanted to see him," Max informed him. Rolling her eyes. "You don't think he's in trouble again, do you?"

"With him, it's hard to tell. But it certainly wouldn't surprise me at all." Frank replied.

"You sure you didn't hear anything about why he was called in, did you?" Max asked.

"Nope, and that's a little strange," he told her, pondering the implications.

Just as he said that, Max's phone rang. Answering it, she heard her boss on the other end. "Somers, get into my office, now," he barked, his anger obvious through the sound of his voice.

"Yes sir," she answered him, not sure why he should be mad at her.

"The boss sounds really irritated. I have to wonder what Murphy did to get his dander up?" She told Frank.

"With Murphy it's hard to tell, but you best get to his office quick, and find out," he advised her.

Max nodded her head in agreement, and quickly headed to O'Brien's office. Arriving, she saw his door open and Murphy leaving, apparently upset. "What's up," she asked him as he was exiting the office.

"You'll find out soon enough. After you're done here, met me at my desk. I got some news for you," he told her.

*I guess that means I'm not getting fired,* she thought to herself, relieved.

"Get in here Detective Somers," O'Brien growled through the open door.

Entering his office, he told her to close the door behind her.

"Am I in trouble, Sir?" She asked.

" Yes and no," O'Brien snapped, continuing. "I need to discuss a couple of issues with you. First, Murphy told me that you made a break in your murder case and that you 'll have it wrapped up today or tomorrow. Is that right?" O'Brien stated to her.

Max paused for a moment, contemplating the implications of her answer. Then she responded, "Yes, I think we have a major break in one of the murders but we still don't have all the answers yet. There is still much we need to figure out to break the case. I think and hope that by the end of today, we will have most of the answers."

"Good, now for the second issue. I see you cleaned up pretty good for your date with the county Coroner, so I've decided to put you on undercover duty for prostitution stings through the SVU department. You obviously got the looks, and I think you're emotionally cut out for it. As a career move, you're perfect for the operation," O'Brien told her firmly.

Max felt her stomach drop. This was the last thing she wanted to hear from her boss. She started to say something but O'Brien cut her off by saying, "No discussion, my mind is made up. I'm cutting the paper work today, so get your case cleared up. Now get out there and do your job. Solve this damn case," he demanded.

Max left O'Brien's office dejected and defeated. Part of her wanted to cry and another part of her was mad as hell. Arriving at her cubicle, she saw Murphy at his desk.

"Well, did O'Brien give you the news?" He asked.

"Yeah, finish the case and get transferred to SVU. No discussion, no choice," she told him.

'I guess he left out the part where he asked for me to put in my retirement papers, didn't he?" Murphy replied.

"He sure did. Why would he ask you to do that?" Max inquired.

"I don't know. Maybe it was because I had too many lunches and bad buffalo wings" Murphy retorted with a smile.

Max smiled back at him, "You think?" She replied, continuing, "I guess we need to finish up this case and see where the cards fall."

"I suppose you're right. So, we go interview wife number one?" Murphy asked.

"Yup, Wife number one. I got her address and have set up a time for an interview this morning. Are you ready?" She asked Murphy.

"Ready," was Murphy's response.

The drive to Mrs. Lewis' nursing home was conducted in complete silence. Both Max and Murphy were wrapped up in their own thoughts about the future of there lives, now that O'Brien had changed their futures.

Arriving at the care facility, Max thought the grounds looked more like a miniature prison rather than a nursing home as she had been informed. There was chain link fencing topped with barbed wire surrounding the whole facility. A entrance gate and gate guard appeared to be the only entrance and exit for the facility.

Driving up to the gate and stopping, the guard approached their car and asked for ID's and destination. Murphy and Max flashed their badges and told in they had made an appointment to see Mrs. Lewis. The guard check his clipboard for their names, then told them that they couldn't take their weapons into the facility and asked them to leave them with him, and they could retrieve them when they checked out.

After they gave him their service weapons, leaving their holsters on, the guard directed them to the front office and told them to ask for the director, Mr. Sanders. The guard then opened the gate for them. Max watched as the gate slowly slid open. Once open, they drove through toward the office the guard had pointed out to them. Looking in the rear view mirror, she saw the gate close and lock behind them.

"You got a back up weapon on you?" Murphy asked her.

"Yup, strapped to my ankle. "You?" Max replied.

" I don't leave home without it," he said, as he lifted his pant leg, showing a small caliper pistol holstered to his lower leg.

Driving to the building's entrance and parking, Murphy and Max sat in the car for a moment and stared at each other.

After a few moments, Murphy nodded to Max, signaling that it was time to go in. They both got out of the car and walked through the door not knowing what to expect

Adjusting their eyes to the dimly lit entrance room, Max saw the cinder block room was painted a dull gray and completely bare of furnishings except for a guard sitting at a gray metal desk. Besides the door they had just walked into, there was only one other steel door providing exit to the room.

The guard looked up at them irritated at being interrupted from looking at his cell phone and demanded, "Business?"

Murphy and Max produced their badges and ID's. When the guard saw their badges, he visibly relaxed. "How can I help you?" He asked much more cordially.

"We're here to see a patient, a Mrs. Lewis," Murphy explained.

"I called earlier this morning and talked to a Mr. Sanders about setting up a visit. It should be cleared," Max interjected.

Hearing that information, the guard spoke into the two way communicator holstered on his belt. After talking to someone on the other end, he informed them that Mr. Sanders would be with them in a minute or two.

It didn't seem to take long before Max heard the lock on the steel door turn and then open. A skinny, pale, balding man with thick glasses entered the room.

"Detective Somers?" He asked, looking at Max.

"Yes," she replied, continuing. "This is my partner, Detective Murphy."

The man shook Murphy's hand. Max noticed that he didn't shake hers.

"I'm Derick Sanders and I am the director of this facility. How can I help you?" He asked them.

"As I explained on the phone to someone earlier, we need to interview Mrs. Lewis concerning the recent death of her ex-husband," Max explained.

"Before we go in, I'm going to ask you conceal your badges. I don't want any of our patients who might see them and get upset." Sanders explained to them and then opened the steel door and ushered them into a dimly lit, long, stark, gray corridor. Max could hear yelling and screaming coming from behind some of the metal doors as they walked down the hallway. As they walked along, both of them moved their badges into their pockets and out sight.

"What kind of nursing home is this? It looks more like a prison." Murphy asked.

"Nobody told you what this facility is?" Sanders asked.

" We were led to believe that Mrs. Lewis was in a nursing home," Murphy told him.

"Well, I guess you could call this a nursing home. A nursing home for the criminally insane." Sanders explained.

"I thought she had tried to commit suicide?" Murphy asked, puzzled.

"She did, by trying to burn her house down with her family asleep inside." Sanders told them, continuing. "Mr. Lewis had a lawyer declared her mentally and criminally insane and the judge sent her here. That was almost seven years ago."

"Is she able to answer questions?" Max asked.

"Oh yes, she's perfectly cognizant of her surroundings and and can communicate just fine," he told them, as he stopped at a metal door. Taking out a ring full of keys, he used one to unlock and open the door. "There's a button located next to the door. Just push it when you're ready to leave," he told them. Then addressing Mrs. Lewis, told her, "Marsha, you have some visitors to see you." As the three of them went into the room, Max saw a middle aged, white haired, matronly woman, who looked like someone's grandmother.

"Thank you, Derick. Will I see you later?" She asked.

"You sure will. Maybe we can finish our chess game later?" Sanders replied to her.

"Okay, I'll see you after supper," she responded happily.

Sanders then left the room, leaving Max and Murphy alone with Mrs. Lewis. As Max heard the lock being turned in the door, sealing them in, Max took a deep breath and looked around the room. It wasn't like anything she had expected.

There wasn't any windows in the room but there was a queen size bed with with silk sheets turned down and a plump comforter covering them. The walls were painted a pastel color, and covered with, what looked like, very expensive oil paintings. A large flat screen television was predominate in the room and a large floor to ceiling bookcase containing books and magazines along with several framed photos of what appeared to be a young Ross and Lisa. In the middle of the room were two upholstered chairs with a chess board between them,

"Mrs. Lewis saw the look on Max's face and explained to her. "It helps to have money, Darling," continuing. "What can I do for the police, today?" She asked,

"How did you know that we're police?" Murphy asked.

"I can see the bulge under your jackets that probably is from your empty holsters, and you sir, have scuff marks on you belt where you obviously usually carry your shield," she observantly told them.

Max was amazed that the elderly woman before them had the mental ability to figure out by simple clues, that they were police and the fact she was committed to a mental institution some how seemed ludicrous. Max knew she would have tread lightly when questioning her. She hoped Murphy would follow her lead and keep his mouth shut.

"Very good observation, Mrs. Lewis. Yes, I'm Detective Somers and my partner is Detective Murphy. If you wouldn't mind, could you answer a few questions for us?" Max asked.

"I suppose it about the death of my ex-husband and his slut of a wife," she commented.

"How did you know." Max asked.

Nodding at the television, she replied, "It's all over the television the last few days. So,tell me, what do you want to know?" She asked.

Max got out her notebook and started asking her the list of questions for her.

" Can you tell me more about all the turmoil many years ago that prompted so many police calls to you and your ex-husband's house." Max questioned, cautiously.

"That was a long time ago, my dear," she replied. " A very long time."

# Chapter 14

"I'm not sure where to start," she told them, tears starting to well up in her eyes.

"Take your time and start at the beginning." Max advised her.

"Of course, my dear. That's always the perfect place to start," she replied, she then wiped the tears away with the sleeve of her blouse.

"The relationship of our marriage was perfect from day one. We were in love and had a great relationship, and eventually, two beautiful children. Our marriage lasted for over twenty years. It wasn't until our business became very successful and went public on the stock market, coinciding with Henry going through a mid life crisis, that the problems began.

It was when he became infatuated with his new company attorney, and started a relationship with her for awhile, that the trouble really began. Something changed in Henry. I think it was the fact that a younger woman was interested in him, or more probably, in his money/

After that, he hardly paid any attention to me or the kids, and that's what really hurt all of the family the most.

Lisa started acting out and having trouble in school and at home. Ross just became distant from everyone. It seemed that Lisa was trying to pay a lot of attention towards her father. More than I was comfortable with. My therapist told me that she was probably trying to fix his lack of attention toward her by over compensation. Several times I found Henry and Lisa in her bedroom alone. When I confronted him about it, he told me that he was just comforting her about her problems at school or helping her with her homework. I knew he was lying but I never could prove anything. Lisa just withdrew farther and farther away from me.

Ultimately, my husband started cruising bars and God knows where else, looking for different companionship. Our marriage was on the rocks and I eventually left him. Ross was starting at the university and lived on campus, but Lisa continued living at home. I have no idea what went on in that house, once I left, but I think I can guess.

I don't know where he found her, but one day he brought his new floozy home and married her. That's when Lisa completely went off the tracks," she explained to Max and Murphy.

"You didn't explain how you ended up here," Murphy asked plaintively.

"No it doesn't, does it," Mrs. Lewis replied, tears welling up in her eyes again.

Wiping away the tears once again, she continued. "It seems that Henry and his new wife supposedly had a major fight and she had left the house overnight to cool off. Henry called me and and told me he was at the house alone. I had told him previously that I would never enter the house if she was there. He then asked if I would come over and see if we could work out an amicable settlement concerning the business.

Like a fool, I took him up on his offer. While we were working out the settlement, he kept plying me with wine. By the time we finished, it was late and I was drunk.

Henry managed to sweet talk me into staying the night, and before I knew it, I was in his bed. The next thing I know I was awoken by the smell of smoke and found the bedroom on fire. Henry appeared with a fire extinguisher in his hands, and proceeded to put out the fire on the rug and drapes.

The fire alarm went off and the fire department arrived and investigated. The investigation eventually was ruled as arson, and I was accused of setting it. It seems that the outside security camera apparently showed someone who looked like me going into the garage and returning to the house with a gas can in my hand," she explained.

" The next thing I know, I was arrested and eventually, with the help of his bimbo company lawyer, I was committed here," she told them.

"You didn't start the fire?" Murphy asked.

"No, not that I remember, but then I was pretty drunk. The police said my finger prints were on the gas container found in the garage, but I have no memory of leaving the bed room that night and going down stairs to the garage, or of lighting a fire," she said. " At the trial, my husband had his company lawyer defend me, but she did more harm to my case then good. She negotiated a plea deal where I was committed here for as long as I am certified insane. My next sanity hearing is early next year, by the way. Derick told me that he was confident that with his recommendation, I should be getting out of here." she told them.

"Your lawyer was Francine Jackson?" Max asked.

"Why yes. Is that bad?" Mrs. Lewis replied.

" May I recommend you get a different lawyer when you have your next hearing" Max advised.

"Why is that, dear?" Mrs. Lewis asked, puzzled at Max's statement.

"Let's just say there might be a conflict of interest. She told us, when we talked to her, that you were almost catatonic and unable to give us a statement. I now have observed that her statement was far from the truth. I have to wonder why she would do that." Max explained. *And what other things did she lie about,* she wondered to herself.

Mrs. Lewis was silent for a moment, contemplating what Max had just told her. "So you don't think she has my best interests in mind, do you?"

"No, based on what you just told me I don't. I don't know what her agenda is but I definitely don't think she has your best welfare at heart." Max told her, continuing, "but I do have one additional question for you."

"Ask away, my dear," Mrs. Lewis replied.

"At the time of the fire, who else was in the house?" Max questioned.

"I think it was just Henry, Lisa, and myself," she responded.

"No Ross?" Murphy asked,

"I don't think so. To the best I can remember, I think he had just started at the University then," she informed him.

" One last question, if you don't mind," Max requested.

"Of course, my dear," Mrs. Lewis told her.

"Okay, do you still have any control over the business and when you're released from here, are you going to take back management of the company?" Max inquired.

"Well since I never signed any agreement with my late husband about the company, because of my being arrested, I'd have to say yes, and I promise you that I know of at least one person in the company who'll be out of a job. Do I make myself clear?" Mrs. Lewis responded vehemently.

"Perfectly clear." Max replied.

"Now I hate to say this, unless you have anymore questions, I think it's time for my lunch to be served and I am a little tired. So unless you want to join me in the wonderful cuisine served here, I think we're done," Mrs. Lewis told them with a warm smile.

Max looked at Murphy with a questioning look and Murphy just shrugged his shoulders indicating he had no more questions for her. Max told her that they were through and thanked her for her time. Murphy went over to the door and pushed the button on the side of the door. It didn't take but a minute or two for a guard to arrive and unlock the door for them.

As they were leaving Mrs. Lewis' room, Max thanked her again and requested she notify her when the competency hearing was, so she could act as a witness for her. Max left one of her cards on the small table next to the door.

Once she and Murphy were out of her room, the guard locked the door behind them and escorted them to the bleak gray receiving room. From there they went back to the parking lot and proceeded to the main gate. Retrieving their weapons, they began the drive back to the precinct. As they rode back, Murphy asked Max, "Well, what do you think."

Max was silent for a few moments, then replied. " If what Mrs. Lewis told is true, and I think it is, then the first thing

I think is she was set up for the fire by her husband and Ms. Jackson, in order to get her out of the way, so they could take over the business, and second, I'm pretty sure Lisa lied to us. I think the person she was writing about in her diary wasn't her brother but her father. I think we need to call Lisa back in for another interview, with more questions about her and her father's relationship. What do you think?"

Almost immediately he responded, "I wholeheartedly agree with both of your assessments, but it still doesn't bring us any closer to who killed our four victims, does it."

"You're right about that, but it certainly does fill in some holes concerning the family dynamics, doesn't it?"

"It surely enlightened me, that's for sure. Talk about a messed up family." Murphy observed.

They rode along in silence for awhile until Max asked Murphy, "Do you think we'll need any back-up executing the search warrant?"

"Not a bad idea. When we get back I'll get some manpower to come with us. I'm sure O'Brien will authorize it." he said.

"And if he doesn't?" Max asked.

"Well, what he doesn't know won't hurt us, right?" He told her with a grin.

"I guess so," she commented.

"After all, what's the worst he can do? Fire me or make me retire and put you out on the street, arresting hookers and johns for SVU?" Murphy told her. The comment brought a smile to her face. Then she just started laughing, which caused Murphy to start laughing too.

Arriving back at the precinct, Max and Murphy split up. Max to eat her lunch and Murphy going to arrange for backup with O'Brien. After about an half an hour, Murphy found Max in the break room. "Are you eating lunch before we go arrest Ross?" Max asked him.

"Nah, I'll eat something when we get back from the university," he responded.

Max just shrugged her shoulders and asked, " Get us any help?"

"Yeah, O'Brien gave us two officers to go along with us. Are you about finished so we can take off?" Murphy asked.

Max stuffed the last of her chips into her mouth and said, "I need a few minutes to take care of some business down in booking. It won't take but about fifteen minutes, okay?"

"Okay rookie, but don't take too long. I'm not getting any younger," he replied.

Max assured him she would be quick, and headed to the elevator. Arriving at booking. She inquired about Pam Harris' cell number. Getting the number, she found her cell quickly in the women's section. There were two other women being housed with her in the cell.

Pam was sitting in a corner of the cell, away from the other two women. Max thought she looked like somebody had roughed her up. Seeing Max, she jumped up and rushed to the bars, and exclaimed, "Detective Somers, I'm so glad to see you. Can you help me?"

Max felt sorry for her, but decided to stand firm and not make any promises to her.

"What happened, Pam? I thought I told you to stay in your apartment?" She admonished her.

"I know you did but I needed a fix real bad and I thought I could score something quick and get back to my apartment quickly before you found out, but it doesn't look like like it worked out to good for me, does it?" Pam told her.

"No, it sure doesn't," Max assured her.

Pam was silent for a few moments, contemplating her situation, then asked the question Max was waiting for. "Look, is there anything you can do to get me out of here? I promise I'll do everything you tell me. Please, you got to help me," she begged, looking sideways at her two cell mates.

Max realized that Pam needed to stay right where she was in her cell and knew fully well that she only wanted out so as to try and buy more drugs, but she felt she needed to do something to help alleviate Pam's situation, so she made Pam a promise she knew she could keep with a clear conscious, " Okay Pam, I'll try to get you out of this cell," she told her.

"Oh thank you, thank you so much," Pam told her, brightening up immediately. Reaching through the cell bars, Pam took Max's hands and squeezed them.

"I'll talk to the booking sergeant on my way out, I promise," Max told her.

Max removed Pam's grip from hers and headed back to the booking area and stopped at the sergeant's desk and asked if he could put Pam in an empty cell if he had any empty ones available. He told her that they were transporting the group of women to Central for arraignment in court in less then an hour and that Pam would be in that group. She figured that Pam could survive for another hour where she was, so told the sergeant to forget her request.

Leaving the holding cells, she headed back upstairs to meet with Murphy. Finding him at his desk, she asked, "You ready to go?"

"Sure am. I think it's time to put this case to rest. You driving or am I?" Murphy told her.

"I'll drive. You look like you could use some rest," she told him with a smile.

"I got the search warrant and I'm calling to arrange to meet our backup there. So let's get this done," he replied, eagerly.

They proceeded to the parking garage and headed to the university to execute the search warrant on Ross Lewis. Arriving at the university research department, they found the two backup officers waiting for them. It only took a few minutes to find Ross working in his lab. Seeing the four police officers waiting for him, Max thought he seemed shocked at seeing them and then upset as he slowly exited the lab to meet them.

"How can I help you officers?" He asked with a false sense of courage.

Murphy started, " I need to inform you that I have an arrest warrant for the murder of Mary Lewis and the subsequent death of her unborn child. We also have a search warrant to search your laboratory and residence. You have the right to stay silent, that any thing you do say can be used against you and you have the right to an attorney. If you can not afford one, an attorney will be provided. Do you understand your rights?"Murphy stated, as one of the backup officers put a pair of handcuffs on him.

Ross remained silent as the reality of his arrest sunk in. "You have to respond Ross. Do you understand your rights?" Max informed him.

Finally, Ross replied verbally and nodded, choking out a, "Yes."

"Good. Officer, stay with him as we search the lab and his locker." Max instructed one of the policemen. All nodded in agreement as Max, Murphy and the other officer carried out the search, with the remaining officer staying with Ross.

Murphy took the search of the desk, while the officer checked out Ross's locker area. Max went through the rest of the laboratory, searching around several large tanks of liquid nitrogen and cupboards full of medical supplies.

Nothing out of order was found in any of the areas searched, so Ross and the officers headed to Ross's apartment to continue the search. It was but a short drive from the lab facility to Ross's on campus apartment. During the drive, Ross remained completely silent and sullen. Arriving at his apartment, they left him in the back seat of the officer's patrol car with one of the backup officers, as the other three literally tore the apartment apart, searching it for anything incriminating.

Just as they were finishing up the search without any results, and getting ready to leave, the police officer came out of the bathroom with a package that appeared to be an object shaped like a revolver wrapped in plastic wrap and duct tape. "Look what I found taped to the inside of the toilet tank," he informed Max and Murphy with a smile.

Both of them realized that the only reason to store a revolver in a toilet tank was that someone didn't want it found.

"Good job, officer. You were wearing gloves when you removed it, weren't you?" Murphy asked.

"Yes Sir," he replied.

"Good, then bag it and tag it and take it to the car," Murphy told him, adding, "but don't show it to the suspect."

"Understood. Are we done here?" the officer replied.

" I think so," Murphy replied. "I just want to talk to Officer Somers for a minute or two."

"Got it. See you at the car," the officer replied as he left the apartment.

Once Max and Murphy were alone, Max asked him, "What did you find?"

"I'm not sure,. I found a pair of shoes in the closet that matches the ones in the video, but I also noticed that the garbage can in the kitchen had a new bag put in recently, and I was wondering if maybe Ross might have disposed of something in the old garbage bag." He informed Max.

"Worth a look," Max agreed, repeating, "It's worth a look."

The two of them headed out the kitchen back door and found the garbage dumpster next to the ally way. Max flipped the lid open and proceeded to pull out several garbage bags. In the bottom, someone had placed several pieces of metal that appeared to look like a disassembled drill press, only without a motor. "Now why would anybody throw away a perfectly good drill press" Murphy inquired.

Astonished, Max informed him, "That may look like a drill press, but it's not. My dad used to do a lot of target shooting when I was a little girl, and he had one of those. It's a reloading press for making your own bullets. Looks like someone took it apart and planned to use the garbage truck to dispose of it. Fortunately we got here before the garbage people did."

Murphy looked at Max and then looked at the reloading press in the bottom of the garbage dumpster. Putting on a new pair of latex gloves, he told Max, "Time to do some dumpster diving, partner."

"Me or you?" Max asked, full well knowing what the answer was.

# Chapter 15

Arriving back at the precinct, Max thanked the two patrol officers for their assistance and took possession of the gun and the reloading press. While Murphy took Ross to the interrogation room, Max took the evidence to the Forensic department for Gemma to evaluate.

Giving Gemma the gun and the reloading press, she then requested the evidence photos that she had obtained from the hospital video. Obtaining the video and the photos taken from the hospital hallway, she headed to the interrogation room where Ross and Murphy were sitting, silently staring at each other.

Entering the interrogation room, she thought that Ross had a defiant look on his face.

Max sat down at the table and put the file and video tape on the table in front of him. Looking at the evidence file and tape, Ross pushed the items back to Max.

"Why am I here?" He demanded, forcing a cocky, confident attitude.

Max started the video tape camera to record the interrogation and turned on the wall mounted television with the remote control and then put the video into a player hooked up to the television.

The screen displayed the image of the long haired, masked nurse walking into Mary Lewis' hospital room with a cloth covered tray and then walking back out a few minutes later. The nurse then quickly walked down the hallway and disappeared from sight.

"Interesting, but why are you showing me this?" Ross asked, sounding bored.

"Well, let me show you some close up photo's taken from the tape. I think you'll find them a little more interesting," Max told him, taking the close up photo's of the nurse's shoes and then the two photos of Ross and of the fake nurse, placing them side by side for comparison.

As soon as Ross saw the photos, Max thought she saw all the color drained out of his face.

"Got anything to say?" Murphy asked.

Ross sat perfectly still for several moments, staring at the photos in front of him, then turned to Murphy and said. "Lawyer."

With that word, Murphy pulled Ross out of his chair and put him in handcuffs and started taking him to the elevator for a trip to the holding cells. As they were walking out the door, Max asked Ross, "Do you want a public defender?"

"No, get me Francine Jackson, The company lawyer." Ross told her, curtly.

As Murphy took Ross down to the holding cells, Max got on the phone to Francine Jackson and informed her that Ross had been arrested for the death of Mary Lewis. When Max informed her of the arrest, there was dead silence on the other end of the phone. From the ensuing silence, Max thought her connection on the phone had been lost or Jackson had hung up on her, but eventually Jackson responded.

"The murder of Mary Lewis?" She responded incredulously.

"And her unborn child." Max added.

Another long silence ensued, then Jackson responded, "I guess he wants me as his lawyer, right."

"That would be correct," Max replied.

"What has he said to you?" Jackson asked.

"Nothing other than requesting you as his lawyer." Max informed her.

"Good- keep it that way. I don't want anybody interviewing to him until I talk to him first. Got it?" Jackson demanded.

"Understood." Max told her.

" And I want to see all the evidence you have. Is that understood?" Jackson demanded.

"Of course," Max responded. "How long before you get here?" Max asked.

"I need to clear my schedule here first, so it probably will be and hour or so before I can get there." Jackson informed her, "You're still at the Beverly Hills station, correct?"

"Yes, that's correct. You where here before with Lisa. I'm on the top floor of the building. If you would, please see me before you see Ross." Max advised her.

"Will do, and remember, I want to see everything you've got as far as evidence. I mean everything." Jackson demanded.

"Of course." Max replied. "I'll see you when you get here." Max told her, hanging up the phone.

It took Max about forty five minutes to get everything ready for Jackson. After she had everything prepared for her visit, she went looking for Frank. She located him in the copy room making what looked like reams of copies stacked and arranged in neat piles on the tables.

"What's up?" She asked walking into to the copy room.

"Busy work for you know who," he replied to her, continuing, "How is your day going?"

Max updated him on the conversation she had with the first Mrs. Lewis, and the arrest of Ross Lewis for the murder of the second Mrs. Lewis.

"I have a meeting pretty soon with Ross Lewis' attorney. I hope I have every thing on order," she told him.

"Want to go over your evidence with me?" He asked. "I'll do anything to get out of this copy room."

"Great," Max replied, grateful for his volunteering.

By the time that Frank and Max has reviewed her evidence, Max received a call from the front desk that Francine Jackson was on the way up to see her.

"Well, here I go," she told Frank.

"Want me there with you?" Frank asked.

"Thanks, but no thanks. I'm going to have to do this by myself eventually. No time like the present," Max told him.

"I understand," Frank responded, continuing, "But do you mind if I listen in on the conversation through the speaker, just in case you get into trouble?"

"No, not at all. In fact, I'd welcome it," she told Frank as she headed to the elevator.

She timed Ms. Jackson's arrival on the elevator perfectly. As the elevator door was just opening, Max arrived. Leading her to the interrogation room, Max felt butterflies in her stomach.

*Why am I feeling so nervous, she asked herself, I have a good case. Nothing to worry about. Nothing to worry about at all.* She kept thinking to herself.

As she walked into the room, she saw Frank standing outside the room, giving her a thumbs up. She responded by giving it back.

Once the two women were seated, Max thank her for coming in so late in the afternoon and then proceeded to show Ms. Jackson the video tape from the hospital, pointing out to her the shoes the fake nurse was wearing, then showing her the pair of shoes found in Ross's apartment.

"As you can see, they are an exact match," Max informed her.

Then she presented the photo comparison between the fake nurse and Ross's face that Gemma had prepared.

"I'd say that these photos are a pretty good match, wouldn't you?" Max asked her.

Next she showed her the photos of the discovered gun from the toilet tank and bullet reloading press from Ross's apartment and garbage dumpster.

While Max was presenting the evidence, Frank was watching through the one way mirror and listening thought the speaker to Max's presentation, thinking to himself. *Don't show her the best part yet- don't show it to her until the right time.*

Ms. Jackson sat silently the whole time that Max was presenting her evidence. Finally, when Max had finished, she began to speak, "First of all, there must be a half a million shoes in L.A. exactly like the ones in the video. Good luck getting them in as evidence in a trial. Second, the photos are merely speculation. I see no similarity between them and I'm pretty sure I can get them thrown out of court, as well as your gun and the bullet reloading press, Show me proof that they belong to my client. What you have here is all circumstantial. No evidence and no motive.

With that, Jackson rose from her chair and said, "Based upon what I've seen here., I'm going to take my client home now."

Frank was watching and listening attentively, and as soon as he heard Jackson say the word 'Motive,' he wanted to silently scream at Max, *Do it now, drop the last piece of evidence on her.*

Almost as if Max could read Frank's thoughts, she took out the last sheet of paper from the folder and laid it on the table.

"What's this?" Jackson asked inquisitively.

"Motive." Max replied, with a smile.

Picking up the sheet of paper disdainfully, she read it over, then, in shock, sat back down in the chair.

While Frank was enjoying the moment of watching Max presenting the final piece of evidence, Murphy walked up to him and asked, "Have you seen Somers?"

Frank merely nodded at the interrogation room.

"What is she doing in there with Jackson?" Murphy asked.

Frank just smiled and said, "Putting a nail in Ross Lewis' coffin."

Francine Jackson had just had the wind taken out of her sails. She re-read the DNA report a second time, then looked up from the table at Max and stated, "This can't be right. Surely there's got to be a mistake."

"No mistake. Our Forensic department ran it twice to make sure. It seems that Ross Lewis was the father of his stepmother's unborn baby," Max informed her, "How's that for motive?"

"It can't be right," then she blurted out. "I need to see Ross now!" Anger starting to take over her demeanor.

"Of course. I'll escort you to his cell." Max informed her.

As the two of them headed out of the interrogation room, they walked past Frank and Murphy standing out side of the door. Frank gave Max a smile and a thumbs up, while Murphy just scowled. Jackson scowled back at Murphy as she walked by him.

After the women had past by, Frank asked him, "What are you upset about, Murphy? She did just fine."

All Murphy replied was, "She should have waited for me," as he walked away.

Max and Jackson rode the elevator down to the holding cells in silence. Arriving at the floor, Max escorted Francine to the booking desk. Before leaving her there, Max asked the Booking Sergeant when Ross would be transferred to Central for arraignment. The Sergeant informed her that he would be transferred the next morning. She knew that she would have to get the evidence to the District Attorney's Office as soon as possible, so they could be familiar with the details of the case.

Heading back up the elevator, she stopped at Forensics to see if Gemma had any good news for her concerning the gun and bullet press they found at Ross's apartment. Gemma met her as she was just getting off the elevator.

"I was just coming to find you. You saved me a trip," Gemma explained.

"Why? What did you find?" Max asked her.

" Before I tell you, could you answer a question for me?" Gemma asked.

"Sure- If I have an answer I can give you." Max replied, puzzled.

"Although both the gun and the bullet press were wiped clean of any finger prints, both of them had high concentrations of nitrogen infused into the metal," Gemma revealed to Max. So my question is, was their any source of nitrogen found in your suspect's apartment or work?

" Not in the apartment but his work lab is full of canisters of liquid nitrogen. Why is that important?" Max inquired.

" Why? No idea how it happened, but nitrogen has broken down the temper of the steel in both the gun and the press. It's almost like they were frozen in liquid nitrogen. If that's the case, I'm starting to form a theory about how your murders took place. But the first I needed to know was if Ross Lewis had any source for liquid nitrogen?" She inquired.

Max pondered, "Yes, like I said, he uses it in his organ research lab at the University."

"That makes perfect sense, but to prove my hypothesis, I'm going to have to obtain a canister of liquid nitrogen for myself, and run a test." Gemma informed her.

"How long will this test take? I have Ross sitting down in holding, waiting to be transferred for arraignment, probably sometime tomorrow morning.' Max informed her.

"You might want to delay his arraignment for a day or two, if you can," Gemma suggested.

"Do you know how much grief I'll get by delaying his arraignment?" Max asked.

"Don't you have seventy two hours that you can hold him before transfer?" Gemma inquired.

"Yes, yes I do," Max replied, steeling herself for the repercussions that would follow.

"I pretty sure I can make it worth your time, if you can delay his transfer," Gemma told her.

"Okay, I'll go back and tell the booking officer to delay the transfer on him. I hope I won't regret it." Max informed her.

"You won't. If I'm right, you'll be thanking me," Gemma promised her.

Max took her at her word and went back down to booking and told them to hold Ross's transfer until she notified them other wise.

The next morning, Max arrived at work feeling relatively calm. Murphy was in the break room, spinning some tale of his to a couple of other officers. Frank was at his desk doing paperwork. Max settled in at her desk to get caught up with some paperwork.

After about an hour, Frank appeared at her desk to inform her that O'Brien wanted her in his office.

*"It must be about Ross' transfer.* She thought to herself. She immediately stopped what she was doing and headed towards O'Brien's office. Arriving, he saw her approach and waved for her to come in to his office. "You wanted to see me, Chief?" she asked.

"Yes. Come in and sit down. We need to talk." O'Brien told her.

Max obediently sat on the chair immediately in front of his desk.

"I hear you've had a break in your murder investigation. Is that correct?" He inquired.

Max took a breath of relief, knowing she wasn't in trouble, and answered, "Yes, that would be correct. We have the step son, Ross Lewis, in a holding cell right now, for the murder of his step mother, and he's possibly involved in the other three,too," she explained to him.

"Well I just had a call from his lawyer who is upset because he wasn't sent over for arraignment this morning. Any explanation?" O'Brien asked,

"Yes, Sir- Forensics is working on new possible evidence that we found at his apartment yesterday. We should have confirmation some time this afternoon, that is, if everything works out," Max assured him, continuing, "Besides, we have seventy two hours that we can hold him before , don't we?"arraignment Max replied.

"Yes, but it's common practice to notify the defendant's attorney that you're holding their client awhile before arraignment. You might want to call her back and let her know the status of Mr. Lewis, as soon as possible," he informed her.

"Did she call you?" Max questioned.

"Yes she did, and she's not very happy. So call her back and get off of mine. Got it?" He snapped.

"Yes Sir," she replied, rising and heading for the door. As she reached the door to leave, O'Brien stopped her when he stated, "Good job. Please keep me updated on your findings, Detective Somers."

Stepping out of the office, she paused for a moment, took a deep breath of relief and then walked back to her desk. Making the phone call to Francine Jackson was a call she really didn't want to make, but she knew it was needed to be done.

The conversation went just about the way she expected it to. Jackson was upset, Max apologized, and informed her the Ross would be at arraignment the next morning. Jackson threatened to get a judge involved if he wasn't.

Hanging up the phone, she took a big sigh of relief, knowing she had bought one more day to find out Gemma's results. She hoped that it possibly could break the whole case wide open.

# Chapter 16

Taking a break after the phone call to Jackson, Max went down to the holding cell and informed the officer in charge that he should continuing to hold Ross for arraignment until the following day. Figuring it was still too early to see if Gemma had found anything out about her case, she went to her desk and went on line to see what happened to Pam Harris at her drug possession arraignment. To her amazement, she saw that the judge had released her on bail until her trial date. *I wonder where she got the money for her bail? I'm guessing she'll be back at her apartment tonight,* she thought to herself.

A little after twelve, Max got a call from Gemma in Forensics, asking her if she could come by the lab in an hour or so.

"Did you find something?" Max asked.

"I think so, but I won't know for sure until after you get here. I'm going to need your help in conducting this experiment. Are you up for it?" Gemma asked.

"Hell yes! I'll see you in an hour and I'll help in any way I can." Max enthusiastically replied.

"Great- see you in an hour." Gemma responded.

The next hour seemed like an eternity to her. To help pass the time, she found Murphy and Frank and told them about Gemma hopefully solving part of their case. She asked Murphy to come along with her, Frank volunteered to also come along also.

An hour later, the three of them rode the elevator down to Forensics together. Arriving at Forensics, they found Gemma and Phil waiting for them.

"I brought some extra help," Max told them,

"Great!" Gemma replied, continuing, "We can use all the observers as possible."

As they walked into the lab, Max was amazed at the transformation that had taken place there. There was several canisters with labels marked as liquid nitrogen, along with several ice coolers scattered through out the lab. Max saw a large metal box set up at the far end of the lab. What it was for, she had no idea. She figured that Gemma would explain it all to them.

When everybody was situated in the lab, Gemma began explaining the experiment, almost sounding like a teacher lecturing her students. "The problem is, how to shoot somebody with out using bullets. The answer is- by using water."

With this statement, the three of then looked at each other with puzzled looks on their faces. Gemma continued, " Now watch as Phil takes the bullet mold, fills it with water and while wearing insulated gloves, immerses the mold into the liquid nitrogen canister."

As she spoke, Phil took a bullet mold and fill the open space of the mold with water. Putting on a pair of thick insulated gloves, he attached a metal clamp onto the bullet mold and immersed it into the open canister of liquid nitrogen. After about thirty seconds, he removed the mold from the canister and placed the mold into one of the nearby coolers. He repeated this procedure five more times.

Gemma then explained what they were doing, "Phil is freezing the water in liquid nitrogen at three hundred and twenty degrees Fahrenheit below zero. This low of a temperature turns the water into ice that has the density of steel. I believe that this frozen ice bullet was used to kill our victims."

"Wait a moment. Even if you were able to make and load a bullet out of water, and fire it, which I don't think you can, then the ice bullet would shatter or melt even before you load the shell casing," Murphy questioned.

"Murphy, you're partially right," Gemma countered, "But watch what Phil does." Nodding to Phil for him to continue. Phil then took a ladle and extracted the liquid nitrogen and poured it into a steel pan sitting on the counter. He then placed the bullet reloading press into the pan of nitrogen. Gemma then produced a box of bullets for them to see.

"These bullets are the same caliber as the gun found in Ross's apartment, I've removed the lead bullet from the casings of six of them. Now Phil, see if you can load one of the bullets you made into one of the empty casings," she instructed Phil.

Even wearing his thick insulated gloves, he easily used a pair of kitchen tongs to pick up one of the ice bullets from the cooler, placed it into the bullet holding mechanism, and then using the same tongs, placed the bullet casing into the loading press.

When everything was aligned, he pulled the handle on the loader, compressing the ice bullet into the casing. Taking the bullet out of the loading mechanism with the tongs, he put the completed bullet back into the same cooler containing the liquid nitrogen.

"Before you got here, we made about twenty ice bullets for the demonstration," Gemma explained, showing them the bullets situated in a case in the same cooler.

"How are you keeping them frozen?" Frank asked.

"Good question. There is liquid nitrogen in the cooler keeping them frozen," Gemma explain to them.

"From here on, we're not sure if this will even work, so we are in unknown territory here," she told them. Gemma went over to a drawer, unlocked it and took out a Colt forty five revolver, similar to the one found in Ross's apartment. Then she brought it over to Phil, who, again using the tongs, easily loaded the ice bullets into the revolver. He then placed the loaded revolver into the same cooler as the ice bullets resided.

"We are cooling the revolver and bullets with liquid nitrogen, down to the same temperature, similar if someone was transporting it to the crime scene," Gemma explained.

While they were waiting for everything to cool down, Gemma and Phil, produced a large block of ballistic gel, and loaded it into the large metal box. When they had finished, Gemma went over to the cooler containing the revolver. Putting on the insulated gloves, she took the revolver out of the cooler, and walked over to the box, Putting on a pair of protective goggles and hearing protections, she advised Max and the men to do the same. The observers immediately complied. Gemma placed the gun through a small opening in the box, aimed at the gel and pulled the trigger.

Max barely heard the click of the mechanism of the gun's trigger as it was cocked into the firing position. Her hopes of finally solving her murder case were riding on the pull of that trigger. Expecting the gun's upcoming explosion, she waited in anticipation. But all she heard through her ear protection was a muted click as the hammer hit the bullet .

Gemma pulled the trigger on the gun five more times, all resulting in five more clicks. Max's hopes were dashed more and more with each resounding click of the gun.

Taking off her ear protection, she asked,"What happened?" Max pleaded, "I thought for sure this world work." she questioned. Her despair sounding in her voice.

Gemma just smiled and told Max, " I suspected that it wouldn't work. The liquid nitrogen is so cold that the firing primer in the bullet can't generate enough heat to ignite the gunpowder."

"Is there a solution?" Murphy asked.

"Of course," Gemma responded, "Don't worry. I have a backup plan." Taking the revolver, she placed it in the third cooler. Closing it up, she explained to them. "This third cooler contains a block of dry ice, solid carbon dioxide. Dry ice is cooled carbon dioxide gas that solidifies at one hundred and ten degrees below zero, Fahrenheit. Unless I'm wrong, I'm hoping that is warm enough to ignite the firing primer and yet keep the bullet from melting. We just need to wait a few more minutes."

After ten minutes of waiting, Gemma put on the insulated gloves and went over to the cooler, extracted the revolver and went back to the box. Again placing the revolver in the small opening of the box and aiming at the carcass, pulled the trigger. The resounding explosion in the the lab was deafening, but to Max, it was the sweetest of sounds. Gemma pulled the trigger five more times, each time Max just smiled more and more with each retort.

Finally, after the gunfire ceased, Gemma and Phil removed the ballistic gel from the box and displayed it the Max and the others.

"Well, that worked. Now to see if we have a match to the wounds on our victims," Gemma told the group. While Phil used a hair dryer set on high heat on the holes of the gel, Gemma went to her desk, brought a photo of a wound on the body of Mr. Lewis and held it next to one of the wounds on the ballistic gel, They appeared identical.

Gemma obtained a medical probe and opened up the ice bullet wound on the pig.

"Notice the ripping and tearing of the tissue of the pig. I can't say for sure, but I'll bet a weeks wages that it's an exact match to the wounds on your victims, And notice- the bullet has melted, leaving no trace," she told them.

"How long would the ice bullets last before they melted?" Frank asked.

"That's just it, the gun has to be cooled or the bullets would melt away in five to ten minutes or less. But with the gun cooled in the dry ice, maybe fifteen to twenty minutes." she explained. If the bullets are made with dry ice, they will shatter and melt when they are fired, but bullets made with liquid nitrogen still retain the tensile strength of steel, even if placed in dry ice.

"Long enough to kill four people?" Murphy asked.

"Definitely yes," Gemma responded, "That's probably why the bullet didn't kill Mrs. Lewis outright. She was shot last and the ice was probably already degrading. That's also why there were no bullets in the wounds. They just simply melted away."

Max, Murphy and Frank just stood in silence for several moments, until Murphy asked, "Will this stand up in a court of law?"

"I've recorded this whole experiment on video, and I have the metal analysis of the gun and reloading press, showing they were subjected to sub-freezing temperatures. So yes. I believe this will hold up in court. Unfortunately both the revolver and reloading press were wiped clean on any fingerprints, so I can't link them to anyone specific. That's your job," Gemma told them.

The three of them were satisfied with Gemma's demonstration and were leaving when Max turned to Gemma and thanked her for all her work. "No problem. Just doing my job," Gemma replied with a smile.

As the three of them rode the elevator back up to their office floor, Frank commented, "Well, that was interesting. What did you think Murphy?"

"I think I have a new respect for the Forensic Department. That's for sure." he replied.

All Max could do was smile at his comment, then asked," Well, now we know how, but we still don't know who or why? Ross has an air tight alibi, but we know he was involved some how. What we need to know now is who pulled the trigger and why,"

Reaching their floor, they exited the elevator.Murphy and Max headed toward their desks and Frank went to inform O'Brien of the progress of the case. Reaching their desks, Max took her notebook and wrote down everything she has seen at Gemma's demonstration. As she was closing her notebook, she saw the initial notes she took from Lisa in her bedroom, on the first day of the murders Something in her notes caught her eye. Re-reading the notes, she looked at her watch. Turning on her computer, she did a quick search. Finding the information she needed, she went and found Murphy.

"Let's go for a drive, Murphy," she asked him.

"Where to?" He asked.

" Let's go to school," she cryptically told him. Murphy just smiled.

Once they were in the car on the street, Max gave Murphy the address of the high school that Lisa Lewis attended. Arriving at the school, Max and Murphy headed to the main office. Once there, they asked for the attendance clerk. The attendance clerk was a little,,gray haired lady that appeared to be over eighty years old.

Showing her their badges, they asked to see the attendance records for Lisa Lewis. The attendance clerk was hesitant to show them the records at first but Max was able to sweet talk her into opening the records to them. It only took a few minutes for Max to find the information she needed.. Thanking the attendance clerk, Max asked her what time is school over. The attendance lady informed then that the release bell would ring in about twenty minutes.

Returning to the car, Max told Murphy to drive them to the student parking lot, which he did. Once parked in the lot, Murphy's curiosity was definitely peeked.

"Okay, what's up?" He asked.

Max just smiled and informed him, "I was looking at my notes and noticed that Lisa told me she left school at three fifteen and arrived home at four. I checked the 911 call time she made, which occurred at four-twenty. Her attendance record for the day of he murder shows that she was marked absent from her drama class, which was her last period. Now the last period lasts for forty- five minutes.

So my question is, what was she doing between two thirty, when she left school early, and when she made the 911 call at four-twenty," she explained to him, finally taking a breath.

"Okay, that's a good catch, but why are we sitting in a student parking lot at the end of a school day?" Murphy questioned.

"Because we're going to find out how long it would take her to drive from school to the house. Just as she said that, the release bell rang, signaling the end of the school day.

The number of students started coming out of the exit door to the parking lot slowly, then turned into a steady stream of students. Max checked her watch, then told Murphy to start driving to the Lewis mansion. She suggested to him to drive the speed limit and no short cuts. When Murphy questioned what she was doing, all Max said was. "Just humor me this once."

Finally pulling up at the Lewis mansion, Max checked the time on her watch.

"Now what?" Murphy asked.

"Back to the office." Max instructed him.

The ride back to the precinct was a silent one. Max was deep in thought as she mulled over the case. What bothered her was the more they discovered about the case, the less it made sense.

# Chapter 17

Arriving back at the precinct, Max proposed to Murphy that they should put their heads together and go over what they had discovered so far. Murphy agreed that it was a good idea. Max felt nervous over Murphy's sudden acts of cooperation

Back at Max's desk, Murphy slid his chair into Max's cubicle and sat down.

"How do you want to go over the case?" Murphy asked her. Letting her take the lead.

"Well, on the detective shows on television, they use a story board to put everything in visual perspective. Do you think it might help us?" Max asked.

"Can't hurt," Murphy stated. "What do we need to do?"

"I'll get photos of everything and everybody that's involved. You find us a presentation board to use." Max instructed.

"That I can do, but look at the time. It's well after five and I got a date with a brew and some buffalo wings," he informed Max.

His mention of a date brought to Max's mind the photo of him with a woman and small boy, that she had found in is desk, when he was on his three day suspension. She decided it was time to question Murphy about it.

"Speaking of dates, I have a personal question for you, if you don't mind?" She asked him hesitantly.

"Sure, but make it quick. I'm not getting any younger," Murphy told her.

"If I cross a line, just tell me it's none of my business," Max replied.

"Yea, yea, just ask the question," he insisted.

"Okay, here goes. When you were on your three day suspension, I looked in your desk for your notebook, and I saw a photo of you, a woman, and a young boy in a picture frame. Can you tell me about them?" Max asked cautiously.

Murphy stared at Max so intently that she thought he was going to hit her. Then his whole demeanor changed. Max could see tears starting to well up in his eyes as he quickly turned his gaze away from Max so as to try to hide his feelings and his tears. Sitting down in his chair, he remained silent for several moments. He then started to speak. "That's my wife and son," he started telling Max. "We got divorced about fifteen or sixteen years ago. She couldn't take being married to a detective who was married to his job, so she left me and took my son with her. I think that's probably when I started drinking," he explained to her.

"Do you keep in contact?" Max inquired.

Murphy replied to her. "Michael, my son, must twenty two years old by now."

"Have you seen him or your ex-wife lately?" Max inquired,continuing, "Has she remarried?"

Murphy became silent, staring into nothing into the air. Then suddenly he rose, shook his head, and told Max, "No."

"Don't you think it's about time?" Max questioned. "Didn't O'Brien tell you to put in for retirement? I think now would be the perfect time to see if you can re-connect with them. Don't you agree? Remember the old adage, nothing ventured, nothing gained."

Murphy was silent for several moments, then calmly replied. "You know, you might be right. I still have her number and address. Guess it certainly does give me something to think about."

The next morning as Max returned to her cubicle, she saw that Murphy had already arrived and had procured from somewhere in the building, a large presentation board on wheels. Murphy told her that Frank has remembered seeing it in one of the storage rooms down in the garage level, complaining it was almost impossible to get into the elevator. Max also noticed that the picture from his desk drawer was now sitting on top of his desk. Seeing the picture, caused her to want to ask about why it got moved, but decided to let it be.

Instead she asked Murphy to roll the presentation board into the interrogation room if it wasn't being used. While he was doing that, she grab a box of push pins, post-it notes and a pile of photos of the people involved in the case.

Meeting Murphy in the interrogation room, she started pinning the photos of the four victims aligned across the top of the board, followed by the photos of Lisa and Ross Lewis. Below them she pinned a photo of Francine Jackson, and next to her photo, placed a post-it note with the word 'Unknown' next to it.

"Who is the unknown person?" Murphy asked.

"Probably our killer, or maybe nobody," Max replied.

"Okay, what do we know about each person?" Max asked.

"Well, everybody on the top row is dead," Murphy quipped sarcastically.

Max gave Murphy a glare and then proceeded to get out her notebook.

Murphy then commented, "I think the gardener and the housekeeper were just collateral damage. You know, wrong place, wrong time."

"Yes but they must have known the killer or killers." Max observed. "So they still are involved." Max said as she placed post-its on the photo, writing 'knew killer' on each one. "What else do we know?" She asked.

"Well, We know that Ross got his stepmother pregnant and probably killed her in the hospital. We also know that he had the gun and the equipment to carry it out. So-motive?" he questioned.

"And the knowledge of how to do it but has an iron tight alibi," Max reiterated.

"What about the girl?" Murphy asked.

"Yeah, what about her? We know she has anger issues from her diary, and that she had a lot of missing time on the day of the murder, but, but again, no motive," Max observed.

"What about Mrs. Mary Lewis?" Murphy continued.

"Young, attractive, gold-digger, and no motive, but most of all, she's a victim. So we can rule her out. She certainly would not hire a hit on herself, would she?" Max replied.

"No, probably not. What about him?" Murphy questioned, tapping the photo of Henry Lewis.

"I don't know. What's your take on him?" She asked Murphy.

" Well," Murphy pondered, "He was rich, successful, likes them young. Did I mention rich?" he said, trying to make a joke.

Max failed to see the humor in Murphy statement. But it started her thinking. Then suddenly it hit her. "Murphy, you're a genius," she said as she started going through her note book.

"I'm glad you finally realize it," Murphy responded, puffing himself up in self assurance. "Wait, what do you mean?"

Max started flipping through her notes then finally found what she was looking for in her note book and read the page to herself.

" You said he likes them young. Do you remember what the first Mrs. Lewis said?

She was upset because her husband was spending a lot of time alone with Lisa. Even in her bedroom," Max revealed.

"You don't think?" Murphy paused.

"I do think, and if I'm right, we might have just found a motive for Lisa." Max expounded, continuing, "And I think we need to talk to her again, and this time we need to take the gloves off."

"I totally agree, and I think we need Ross with her at the same time," Murphy suggested,

"Good idea, and I guess we will have their attorney present too, which is good because I have a few questions for her also." Max replied. " I think we've been lied to throughout this whole case, and I think it's time to get some straight answers."

"Okay then, you arrange to get Lisa and Francine Jackson here after lunch and I'll get Ross Lewis transported over to us as soon as he's arraigned this morning," Murphy suggested.

" Sounds good. I say we schedule the meeting at one o'clock." Max suggested.

"Works for me," Murphy replied to her."

After their conversation, Max made arrangements with Frank to get the interrogation room reserved for them.

After completing that task, she got on the phone to Francine Jackson and informed her that she wanted to interview Lisa and Ross at the precinct at one o'clock that afternoon.

" Concerning what?" Jackson asked.

"What do you think it concerns. The murder of four people. That's what it concerns," Max told her somewhat coldly.

There was a long silence on the other end of the phone. Finally Jackson replied, " I don't think we can make it on such short notice. Perhaps a different day this week might work better."

"I don't think you understand. This is not a request. I will send a couple of officers to bring you here, if needed," Max insisted. "In fact, I think that's a pretty good idea."

Absolute silence followed. "Are you still there?" Max questioned on her phone. Still more silence. "Hello! hello! Can you hear me, Ms. Jackson?"

After several more moments of silence, Max heard the response from Jackson.

"Okay, I'll be there at one o'clock with my client," she replied, then abruptly hung up.

*I guess I must have pushed a few buttons,* Max thought to herself, *Good.*

Max and Murphy had lunch together in the break room where they planed their strategy as far as questioning their suspects. Murphy suggested that he interrogate Ross and Max take Lisa and Jackson,

"Do you think we need to remove the presentation board from the interrogation room?" Max asked,

"Nah, let them see it. It's a good intimidation factor. Let them think we know more than we really do," Murphy replied. Max had to agree.

At a quarter to one, Murphy went down to the holding cells and brought Ross up to the interrogation room. He was surly and silent as he sat in the interrogation room with Murphy. Meanwhile Max was waiting by the elevator, waiting for Francine and Lisa.

It was past one thirty when the two of them stepped off of the elevator. Jackson apologized for being late, saying that heavy traffic had held them up. Max observed a look of terror on Lisa's face. Max realized that it wouldn't take much to break her.

Walking into the interrogation room, Lisa's terror turned to absolute panic, when she saw Ross and the presentation board waiting for them. Max saw the look that Lisa and Ross gave each other. Max caught the look on Murphy's face as they both realized that this could be the big break in the case.

"Okay, why are we here?" Jackson opened. Lisa took Jackson's hand like a child hanging onto their mother for support.

Following their planned strategy, Murphy opened. "We are here to present our findings in the case of the murder of your parents, the maid and the gardener. The evidence we have found, shows that Ross probably manufactured ice bullets using his knowledge of liquid nitrogen, procured a revolver, both items of which were used to murder your father, stepmother, maid and gardener. When the stepmother unexpectedly survived the attack, Ross disguised himself as a nurse, entered his stepmother's hospital room and gave her an injection of air in her IV line, causing her and her unborn child to die."

"And why would he go to all this work to kill his stepmother?" Jackson asked.

"Why? Because the unborn baby was fathered my him. This was verified by a DNA match between the fetus and Ross. Why this happened- no idea, How it happened- basic biology."

When Murphy finished. Max took over. "Lisa. Based upon the evidence we've discovered, we believe that you, taking the revolver and ice bullets prepared by Ross, drove from school to your home, where you shot and killed the gardener and maid because they would be able to identify you, killed your father because he had abused you as a child and probably was still abusing you. Then not finding you stepmother at home, waited for her to return, where you attempted to assassinated her, probably as a favor for your brother.

"This is crazy," Jackson erupted, "You haven't one shred of concrete evidence pertaining to these absurd charges."

As she was contradicting the charges, Lisa, who had a look of panic on her face began having a major meltdown. She turned red in the face, began sobbing hysterically, until she suddenly blurted out in anger to Jackson, "You said if we followed your plan, they would never figure it out. Why did you talk us into doing it? Your just as guilty as we are!"

Murphy and Max just stood there in shock as Jackson turned red in the face and tried to explain to them, " She's just hysterical and in shock. She's been under a lot of stress, what with finding her parents murdered. She doesn't know what she's saying."

Recovering from Lisa's outburst, Murphy immediately informed the the three of them that the interview was over.

"What do we do now?" Max inquired with a whisper to Murphy.

"We separate them and read them their rights," Murphy responded, as he began calling on his phone for reinforcements.

Very quickly there were several officers appearing at the interrogation room. Murphy instructed the arriving officers to remove Lisa, Ross and Peterson to separate holding cells and read them their rights.

Turning to Max, Murphy told her to call social services and arrange for a child advocate and a new lawyer for Lisa, and told her that he was going to call the District Attorney. Max immediately went and made the calls needed. After making her phone calls, Max went and found Murphy sitting reflectively at his desk.

"What's next?" She asked him

"Divide and conquer," he responded. " We interrogate the three of them separately, then piece the information together. We start with the daughter and work backwards. But we can't talk to her until her advocate and lawyer arrive. When did Social Services say they would be here?"

"They can't get anybody here for a couple of hours," Max informed him.

"I guess we're going to be here for awhile. If you got any plans for tonight, you better cancel them," he told her.

"No problem- I have no life outside of work," she replied. Murphy just smiled at her.

It was well over two hours before a Social Services representative and a lawyer arrived, and another forty minutes before they were through talking with Lisa. Once done, they found Max and Murphy and asked to have a conversation with them.

Moving to the interrogation room, Lisa's lawyer started the conversation. "Where are we on charges?"

Murphy replied, "Right now we think she's responsible for three murders and one criminal assault, but it really is up to the District Attorney to decide the final charges."

"And if she cooperates?" The lawyer asked, "You know she's only seventeen."

"Well, she could be charged as an adult. The DA informed me to tell you, her cooperation might tempt him to consider charging her as a minor, but it really comes down to our recommendation,"Murphy informed him.

With that statement, the lawyer and social services advocate huddled together and whispered back and forth until they seemed to finally came to an agreement. The lawyer informed Murphy and Max that if they would recommend the DA to charge Lisa as a minor, then she would cooperate.

Upon hearing the lawyer's statement, Murphy rose from his chair and stated, "Good, let's talk to her now."

# Chapter 18

Max went down to the holding cell and brought Lisa back to the interrogation room. Once every one was settled in their chairs, Max turned on the video camera to record the conversation. Her lawyer started the interrogation by stating his name and telling the camera that his client was a legal minor and making a statement of her own volition.

After making his statement, he signaled to Lisa to start her confession. "My name is Lisa Lewis and I want to confess to my part in the murder of my father, step mother, maid and gardener. I was the one that shot them." After her statement, Max said that they were going to need more details than what she had given them. Lisa looked at her lawyer who nodded for her to continue.

"Okay, when I was eight or nine, my mother and father were fighting a lot and making everybody's lives miserable. That's when my father started doing things, inappropriate things, to me when my mother wasn't around. When he remarried his new girl-toy, everything got better, but eventually even his new plaything wasn't enough, and the abuse started again. When I told my brother what was happening, he went into a rage. That's when he confided to me that when he had came home for spring break and our father was at work, she got him drunk by the pool and seduced him." Lisa confessed to them.

"We knew that we had to get out of that house. That's when Ross told Ms. Jackson what was happening. My brother told me that he told her because she was a lawyer and might be able to legally get me away from them. Ross told me a few days latter, that she came up with the scheme to eliminate the two of them. Once they were gone, she planned to run the company for us, then Ross and I would be free of both of them, and rich enough to do whatever we please." Lisa finished, then began crying again.

As the advocate tried to console Lisa, Murphy whispered to Max, "Step one done, now onto Ross. Do you think we are through with her?"

Max whispered back to him, " I have a couple more questions for her before we start on Ross."

Murphy nodded his head and told her. " Go for it." Max then turned her attention back to Lisa.

"One last question, Lisa. If you don't mind." Max asked, continuing, "How did you get the weapon and the ice bullets from Ross, and what did you do with them after you used them?"

Lisa looked at her lawyer, who nodded his head in affirmation. " Ross and I figured that our stepmothers birthday would be the appropriate time to carry out our plan. So the night before, I drove to Ross's apartment and picked everything I needed, the revolver, the special gloves, and a cooler with the bullets being kept cool with dry ice. Ross told me that I had about fifteen to twenty minutes after they were loaded in the gun to use before they melted. After we carried out our plan, the next day I took the gun and cooler to Ms. Jackson, when

I went to stay with her. Francine told me that she would make everything disappear."

Max was amazed that Lisa was so casual and emotionless, as she calmly described the details of the killing of her father, mother-in-law, maid and gardener, but she realized that Lisa had unwittingly brought up a question that had to be answered.

"So you gave the revolver to your lawyer, who is also your guardian?" Max questioned.

"Yes, why?" Lisa replied.

"Just following the evidence. That's all." Max replied to her. "I guess that's all I need from her, for now," she added.

Once the interview with Lisa was completed, she was taken back to her cell accompanied by an officer and her advocate and lawyer.

Once they had left the interrogation room, Murphy stated, " One down and two to go. I guess we're ready for Ross," Murphy told Max. Max nodded and called down to booking and instructed them to bring him up to interrogation. As Murphy and Max waited for Ross to arrive, they discussed how to question him. Max suggested that Murphy go first and she would finish. Murphy agreed with her.

It took about twenty minutes for the two officers to deliver Ross to them for interrogation. After getting settled in, Murphy began his questioning. " Well Mr. Lewis, I assume you had your rights explained to you, correct?"

Ross just sat silently in his chair. "Let the record show Ross Lewis didn't respond to the question." Murphy stated to the tape recorder, continuing, "We just interviewed your sister with her lawyer and we want to make sure you don't want representation. So one more time- do you want a lawyer."

Ross just sat in his chair, sullen and silent.

Murphy continued, " Okay, here is what we know. We know that you provided Lisa with the revolver and the special bullets that you made in your cryogenic lab which she used to kill four people. We know that you planned with your sister, and with the help of Francine Jackson, your lawyer, to kill the family solely for the money and also to get rid of the woman who got pregnant by seducing you and also to kill the man who was abusing your sister. We know that your mother-in-law, the woman that seduced you, survived the assault and was subsequently killed by you in the hospital.

We also know a good lawyer might argue in court that the evidence of the hospital assault is circumstantial, but taken with the totality of what we have and Lisa's confession, I don't think any jury on Earth would have a tough time connecting the dots."

With that statement, Ross turned ashen white. Max could tell all of his resolve was drained. Finally realizing there was no escape, he asked, "What do you want to know?"

With that statement, Max took her turn in asking questions. "Not what, but who? Who put you up to this plan?"

Ross remained silent for several moments as he weighed his options. Finally speaking in a quiet voice, he told them, "My lawyer, Francine Jackson, the Chief Financial Officer of Lewis Industries."

"What was her part in this crime?" Max asked inquisitively.

Ross hesitated for a moment as he weighted his options, then began his statement. "I believed that Francine groomed

Lisa to commit murder over the last couple of years, about the same time that my dad married that despicable woman.

She drew me into her plan when she found out that my mother-in- law was going to have a baby. Francine told Lisa and me that dad was in the process of changing his will, leaving everything to the slut and the new baby. She told Lisa and me what we had to do and to do it quickly."

"One last question," Max requested.

"Sure." Ross responded to her.

"You know now that when we searched your apartment and found the revolver and eventually showed it to you latter, you looked positively dumbfounded. Why was that?" Max asked.

Ross replied immediately to her, "Because it shouldn't have been there. I purchased the revolver out on the street, gave it to Lisa and she gave it to Francine to get rid of. How it made it back into my apartment, I have no idea, unless..."

"Jackson set you up by planting it in your apartment." Max completed his sentence.

"But why would she do that? I liked her and I thought she liked me,"Ross pleaded to them.

"No idea, but I can guarantee you, I'm going to find out," Max assured him.

Since she had no more questions for him, she asked Murphy if he had any more questions. He shook his head indicating that he was through. Max called for an officer to take him back to his holding cell. After Ross was gone, Murphy quipped, "Two down and one to go."

"How do you want to handle her?" Max asked him.

"Well what we are doing seems to be working. Let's keep doing it," Murphy suggested to her. Max had to agree.

Murphy looked at his watch and told Max, " It's almost six thirty. Do you want to grab some dinner and let Peterson stew for awhile? My treat."

"Great idea, but I'm not going to your regular dinner spot, "Max told him with a smile.

"Fine." he responded, I do occasionally eat at regular restaurants, you know." Murphy told her with a smile. "What do you like?"

"Usually Italian, but I'd settle for fast food," Max informed him.

"Are we in a hurry?" Murphy questioned.

"Not at all. Nope, not at all," Max replied, with a grin.

"Italian it is, then," he told her.

They went to an Italian restaurant a couple of miles away from the precinct. Max was amazed that Murphy didn't have any alcohol during the meal. When Max commented on his abstinence, he smiled at her and told her that he was on the wagon. When Max inquired as to why, Murphy said that he had taken her advice and contacted his ex-wife and son. " My boy is now married and has a child on the way. My ex-wife told me the only way she and my boy will see me is if I quit drinking, so, no more alcohol for me."

"Good for you. I'm really impressed. How do you feel now that you're not drinking anymore?" Max asked.

"I feel like I want a drink. But quitting is long overdue, and I appreciated you for suggesting it," he explained to her, then looking at his watch, informed her it was time to get back to work. With that said, they finished their meal, Murphy paid the bill and they returned back to the precinct building. Once arriving at their desks, Max made the arrangements to get Francine Jackson transferred from holding to the interrogation room. Max reminded Murphy that he better take it easy with his language, as there was still probably a lot of acrimony between Jackson and him. Murphy agreed and pledged to go easy on her and be on his best behavior.

It didn't take long for Francine to arrive at interrogation room. Once settled in their chairs, Max turned on the recorder. That's when Murphy took over.

"Okay Ms. Jackson, we've interviewed Lisa and Ross, and we have a pretty good idea of what went down at the Lewis house. Now we would like to get your side of the story.

Tell me, when did you start forming the plan to assassinated the Lewis' and why?" He asked her, almost cordially.

Francine just sat silently, saying nothing.

Murphy continued his questioning, "As a lawyer, you knew that Lisa probably would be charged as a minor and with her cooperation and her extending circumstances, probably will do minimum time, probably in a juvenile facility. She might even get off with diminished capacity with a good lawyer and a sympathetic judge.

Ross however, will probably face conspiracy charges and possession of a firearm used in a felony, and murder of his mother-in-law, along with lying to the police.

You on the other hand, probably will be charged with conspiracy, grooming of a minor to commit a felony, possession of a firearm used in a felony and a host of other charges."

She still sat silently, not responding to anything Murphy threw at her. Max thought she saw Francine's eyes begin to tear up.

Murphy continued, "Even if you're were possibly found not guilty, I'm sure your job at Lewis Industries will be over as well as your law degree suspended. So again, why?"

She continued to be silent but now the tears began to flow down her cheeks.

Max then took her turn at questioning her. " You purposely planted the murder weapon in Ross' apartment. You knew we would eventually search his place. You wanted us to find it. But why? Why would you go through this charade of setting this whole thing up only to basically give us the evidence to solve it?" Max insisted.

With this last question, Jackson completely lost it. She began to sob uncontrollably, tears streaming down her face, causing her make up to run. Max thought she had finally broke through to her, but the statement Francine finally made was not what she expected.

"Because I was ordered to. I'm being blackmailed," she blurted out, in between sobs.

Both Max and Murphy were both taken aback by her utterance. "Blackmailed?" Max responded. "Who is blackmailing you and why?" she questioned.

Murphy had found a box of tissues that he handed to Francine. After she dried her eyes and became more settled, she began to explain. "About three years ago, I began getting blackmail letters with photos of Henry and me in the pool and hot tub in, how should I say it, very compromising positions.

The letters told me that if I didn't do exactly what I was instructed, that the photos would be released to the Board of Directors of Lewis Industries. Those photos would cost me my job and torpedo any chance of the business going public on the stock exchange.

I was trapped. The letters described exactly what I was to do and how to do it. They told me that I had three years to carry out the scheme. While I was influencing Lisa and Ross to carry out the assassination, Henry went and remarried, which put a new wrinkle in the plan which had to be adjusted for."

"Do you know who was sending the letters?" Murphy asked.

'No idea," she replied, "But who ever they are, they knew a lot of personal details about my life, Henry, Ross and Lisa's. It was almost like they were spying on all of us and knew exactly how easily it was to manipulate us."

"But why leave the revolver in Ross' apartment, where you should have known it would be discovered?" Max asked.

"I was told in the last letter to do it. I guess they wanted to incriminate him too. Because I had the uneasy sensation that someone was watching me, I didn't dare not follow the instructions," Jackson replied. Then she asked, " Am I getting arraigned tomorrow so I can post bail?"

Murphy responded to her question. "It's too late to get our evidence to the District Attorney tonight, so maybe tomorrow morning or the early afternoon. So any way you cut it, you're going to be spending spending the night with us."

As Jackson was escorted back to her cell, Murphy and Max discussed the case back at Murphy's desk.

"Well, that's almost a wrap on the case. Do you think we'll ever discover who was pulling the strings on Jackson?" Max asked speculatively.

"Don't know, but maybe a good night sleep might help us figure out who it is," Murphy told her. "God, I'm tired."

"You know, I was really impressed with the way you handled Jackson. Frank was right when he said you really are a good detective," Max praised him.

"Never any doubt about it, rookie," he responded with a broad grin.

"Did I just hear my name bandied about?" Frank called out as he walked up to them.

"Yes you did, but in a good way." Max replied.

"Hope so," he stated. "Rumor has it that you guys broke your murder case. Is it true?"

"True- we didn't solve it within the deadline given to us by O'Brien but we did finally solve it. It really was a team effort," Murphy informed him, as he started for the elevator.

As the elevator doors closed on Murphy, Frank looked at Max with a expression of amazement.

"You tamed the beast. Way to go," Frank told Max. "How did you do it?"

"I wore him out. By the time he gets a good night sleep, he'll be back to his normal self," she told him with a smile.

"Well, I'll inform O'Brien that the case is closed," Frank told Max.

"Could you just tell him that we have had a major break and are close to finalizing it shortly," Max requested.

Frank gave her a broad smile and asked, "Not ready to go undercover with the pimps and prostitutes?"

"Not really, but it is true, We have the actors in our play, but we haven't figured who the director is." Max explained to him.

"Okay, I can probably gain you a day or two. O'Brien has something going on in his personal life that's taken his attention away from you, so finalize everything as fast as you can," Frank informed her.

"Thanks Frank. I promise I'll keep you informed. It shouldn't take too long. But right now, what I need now is a good night sleep," she told him.

"Go home and get some rest," Frank advised her.

"Okay, I guess the pimps and prostitutes are going to be safe for another night," Max jokingly replied.

"See you tomorrow, then," Frank told her.

"Yes you will," Max informed him.

With that, Max gathered her things and headed home. Arriving at her apartment, she made a quick supper and then made a lunch for the next day. Dead tired, she stretched out on the couch and started mulling over the days proceedings. Rehashing how everything transpired through out the day, she finally ended up with the final question. Who was blackmailing Francine Jackson? Who was the unknown someone who was controlling and pulling the strings that set up the murder of four people and ruined the lives of three others? Who was the unknown individual that knew Jackson, Lisa and Ross so well that they could manipulate them so easily. Then it hit her. She knew of only one person who filled the criteria in all categories. And she also knew that she and Murphy needed to make a road trip the next day.

# **Chapter 19**

Max was early to work the following morning after a good night sleep. Getting off the elevator, she saw Frank carrying a briefcase, heading toward O'Brien's office.

"O'Brien got you running errands this early in the morning?" She asked him as he passed by.

Frank stopped on his way to the office and told Max, " Yeah, the big wigs from central are coming in for a meeting this morning, and he wants these paper delivered to his desk immediately," Frank explained.

"Have fun,"Max kidded. Frank just rolled his eyes and continued his journey. Max smiled and headed to her desk, About a half an hour later, Murphy arrived at his desk.

"I was thinking about our case last night. I think I know who the person behind everything is." she told him.

"Really? Who do you have in mind?" He asked curiously.

"The one person who would know all three of our suspects intimately,"Max informed him,

"Who's that?" Murphy asked.

"Marsha Lewis," Max replied.

"Their mother? No way." Murphy exclaimed.

"Who else would be familiar with her kids, and the affair between Lewis and Peterson. And if you remember, she was familiar with the placement of the security cameras around the residence. What better way to get blackmail photos then off the security cameras," Max explained to him.

"Well, I guess it wouldn't hurt to talk to her again. When do you want to go?" Murphy asked.

"No time like the present. You got anything more important to do right now?" Max questioned.

"Nope, you're right. No time like the present. You driving?" Murphy inquired.

"Sure," Max responded.

It took them about half an hour to get to the facility. Arriving, they checked in at the guard gate and entered into the waiting area. Telling the guard that they were there to see Marsha Lewis, they had to wait over twenty minutes before the director, Derick Sander, arrived and took them to Marsha Lewis's door.

"You know the rules and the procedures. Please don't upset her, and keep it short. She has a therapy session in about fifteen minutes." Sanders told them. He then knocked on the door and said, "Marsha, you have some visitors. Are you dressed?"

Mrs. Lewis replied "Yes." Sanders unlocked the door and invited them in. He then excused himself, telling them that he had other issues that he needed to address immediately, elsewhere. Max and Murphy entered her room and heard the door close and lock behind them.

"So nice to see you two again," She warmly stated. "Did Derick tell you our wonderful news?"

"No, he didn't say anything. Is your hearing coming up?" Murphy asked her.

"I wish, but no. The news is that Derick proposed to me. We're getting married next weekend," she told them, flashing a beautiful diamond engagement ring.

"Well congratulations, but we came here for other reasons. Have you heard that Ross, Lisa and Francine Jackson have been arrested for the murder of your ex-husband and his new wife along with your maid and gardener?" Max inquired.

"Really! Why on earth would they do that?" Marsha asked in amazement.

"Well, Ms. Jackson told us she was being blackmailed to orchestrate the murders. Somebody was sending her photos of your late husband and herself in the pool and hot tube in compromising positions. Would you happen to know anything about that?" Max questioned,

"Oh my goodness dear, no! I knew photos of them existed but they were in the library of the house. My late husband had them made from the security tapes that showed them together. He was extremely proud of them. When I found those disgusting pictures in the house, it was the final straw of our marriage. But I never took any of them and even if I did, how could I even send them to anybody. My incoming mail and all of my correspondence is monitored. I'm not allowed a computer or cell phone in here, so except for my television and my books and a radio, I am isolated from the outside world," she explained to them.

"I guess you make a valid point." Max replied. "You didn't tell anybody about those photo's, did you?"

"No, I'm ashamed to have even seen them. Why would I ever tell anybody about them?" Marsha almost yelled, then paused in reflection, " Wait- I did discuss them once in my therapy session, but that was three or four years ago."

"That was about the same time the blackmail began. Who would have access to your therapy session?" Murphy asked her.

"Well, my therapist, but I'm sure she wouldn't divulge anything, but she does tape our sessions, and the tapes always stay here on the premises." she divulged to them.

"And who has possession of them here?" Max inquired.

"Why, the warden. Derick," Marsha stated. As soon as she said that, the realization of who the blackmailer was, quickly became realized to her. "No-No-No, he couldn't have done it, He wouldn't have done it, we're in love. He gave me an engagement ring. We're getting married next week," she sobbed.

Max and Murphy looked at each other, realizing that they finally knew who was the mastermind behind the blackmail and ultimate murders. Murphy walked over to the door and pushed the alarm button. Max then told Marsha, "I don't think that as a inmate in a mental institution, you can legally marry." With that information, Marsha broke down in tears.

Several minutes later, Derick Sanders unlocked the door and opened it. As soon as he entered, Murphy grabbed one of his arms, pulled it behind his back and proceeded to put handcuffs on him. "Derick Sanders, you are under arrest for blackmail and facilitation of murder," Murphy told him.

Sanders first reaction was one of indignation but seeing the look on Marsha's face, he knew that he had been discovered. A look of resignation quickly followed.

"I did it for you, Dear. I did it so we could have it all after we got married and you're released from this hole.

Marsha just glared at him, slipped the engagement off of her finger and put it in his jacket pocket. "Keep you damn ring. You'll need it to hire a good lawyer," she raged at him.

Max and Murphy began escorting Sanders out of the room when Sanders asked Max to be sure to lock the door of Marsha's room. Max took the door key from his handcuffed hand and locked Marsha's door behind them. The irony of the situation wasn't lost on Max.

After the sound of her door being locked, Marsha quickly wiped her tears away and sat down on the overstuffed chair next to the chess board. Reaching over the chess pieces, she tipped over her opponent's king and simply said, "Checkmate."

Then thinking to herself, thought. *Men are so easy to manipulate. It's almost criminal.*

# Epilogue

Max leaned back in her seat of the airplane she was taking off on from the Minneapolis/St. Paul airport. Her jet was taking off late but she didn't care. She was finally heading back home to her daughter, job and apartment in Los Angeles.

Minnesota was nice, the weather was mild and the people friendly. She thought Minneapolis was a thriving metropolitan city but was so much smaller than what she was used to in L.A.

But what was really small was the quaint town of Royal Oaks, a small town just west of Minneapolis. This had been her destination of her job interview for the detective opening they had on their police force. She had felt the interview went well. Royal Oak's Chief of Police, Chief Paulson, was a real sweet heart. He struck her as somebody's friendly grand father. She felt that if they offer her the position, she could easily work with him as her boss. But living in a small town like Royal Oaks was another matter.

Chief Paulson was a far cry from Chief O'Brien. As soon as she and Murphy had put put their murder case to bed, O'Brien retired Murphy from the force. When Max asked Murphy what his plans were, her told her that he was doing Alcoholics Anonymous, fishing, and was talking with his ex-wife and son, and excitedly preparing to meet his new daughter-in-law and grand son.

O'Brien, true to his word, put Max into a SVU division, working under cover with prostitutes and pimps on the streets of Beverly Hills. Max absolutely hated it.

Frank continued on as deputy chief until Central discovered all of the mismanagement issues that had occurred under O'Brien's watch. O'Brien quietly got demoted and assigned to a different division. She heard through the grapevine that he resigned soon after and retired. Upon his removal, Frank was promoted to department chief.

Max hoped that with Frank's promotion, she might get re-assigned to her old division, but Frank told her that O'Brien had given her such a poor evaluation for not meeting his deadline, that it would be impossible for her reinstated back to Beverly Hills. Trying to help her out of her bind, he found an advertisement for a detective position in the Police Journal at a small town in Minnesota called Royal Oaks. Showing the ad to her, he suggested strongly that she apply for it. He even told her to use him as a referral. When she showed the ad to Murphy, he concurred with Frank and told her to apply. He too said her would recommend her. So she thought, *What the heck. Why not apply. Nothing ventured, nothing gained.* So she did.

Sammy O'Brien got out of rehab and immediately went back to his old life of running drugs. Max heard on the street, that Sammy owed a lot of money to his supplier and then one day just disappeared.

Pam's parents had posted their home to provide bail for her release from jail. Once released though, she never appeared for her court date. Her parents unfortunately lost their home. Max hoped that perhaps Sammy and Pam found each other somehow, and had started a new life somewhere, but she also feared that in reality, they probably were in barrels at the bottom of Mulholland Dam Reservoir. Victims of their chosen life style.

Safely arriving back at LAX, Max turned on her phone to check for messages. There was only one message in her voice mail. It was a voice mail from Chief Paulson, asking her, 'When can you start?'

www.ingramcontent.com/pod-product-compliance
Lightning Source LLC
Chambersburg PA
CBHW051230130726
47988CB00001B/290